Through The Fury of The Storm

His Stormchasers

Book 3

By

Ronna M. Bacon

Proverbs 30:5 Every word of God is pure: he is a shield unto them that put their trust in him.

Psalm 59:16 But I will sing of thy power; yea, I will sing aloud of thy mercy in the morning: for thou hast been my defence and refuge in the day of my trouble.

Table of Contents

Chapter 1

Shrugging deeper into his heavy jacket, Delaney Callahan searched the area of the forest he was in, listening for the barks of his Border collie. Calling for him, he listened again even as he tugged down his knitted hat on his dark blond hair and pulled his gloves on tighter. He squinted at the sky, his deep blue eyes closing against the sting of the snow pellets. They'll be turning to sleet soon, he thought, and began calling once more for his dog.

His head turning, he headed off, slipping and sliding on the icy slope as he searched, not seeing Mick.

"Mick? Where are you, boy? Come on. Let's go. It's time to head for home."

Mick's excited barking had him stopping in his tracks, wavering a bit to keep his footing, before he set off on almost a run. Something was wrong, he thought. Lord, I have no idea what's going on but You do. Let me be Your instrument today.

He slipped and slid towards Mick, finding the dog crouching down and not moving.

"Did you hurt yourself, boy?" He dropped to his knees, his hands reaching for Mick, before his eyes stopped. "What did you find, boy?"

He reached for the pile of snow, brushing it off, his hands freezing as he saw a jacket and then jeans.

"What is this?" He reached to touch the back of the body, whispering a sigh of relief that the person was breathing. He shoved Mick to one side so he could brush away the rest of the snow. "It's a lady, Mick. Now I wonder why she's out here? And on a day like this?" He felt along her arms and legs. "It doesn't look like she's broken anything, boy, but we need to get her home and to Dad's care." He carefully lifted her, her head dropping onto his shoulder, her hood covering her face. "Come on, Mick. You've done good today. She's have frozen to death in a little bit more time. Let's go. Lead on, buddy. I'll follow."

Carefully carrying his burden, he followed his dog, who kept turning to watch, finally dropping back to pace at his side, his eyes on the burden his master carried. Delaney walked as fast as he could, his eyes dropping every once in a while to the lady he carried. Something about her seemed familiar but he wasn't sure even about that.

He struggled to open the door to his parents' kitchen and stepped in, stomping off as much snow and slush from his boots as he could, his mother, Moira, turning in surprise before she was across the kitchen, her hand on her son's arm, her colouring matching his.

"Who do you have, Delaney?"

"I have no idea, Mom." His baritone voice was low, as if he would disturb the lady he held if he spoke too loud. "Mick found her out in the meadow. I don't know how long she's been there, but she hasn't roused at all."

"Here, into the spare room. Your Dad's in the office. Mick, go get Dad."

Mick gave a low woof as if he too needed to keep his bark low and ran for the office, tugging at Graeme's sleeve.

"What's up, Mick? Did Mom send you for me?" He rose, a frown on his face. Mick was agitated and that was unusual for him. He followed the dog as he ran for the stairs and to the spare room where he stopped, chin on the bed, brown eyes fastened on the lady as Delaney laid her down.

"You're soaking wet, son." Moira turned to her son. "Go, get changed. There's fresh tea in the kitchen."

"Thanks, Mom." He hesitated, his eyes on the lady, whose face was still hidden by her hood. "Let me know what I can do to help."

Graeme paused by his son, his frown still in place. "Who's this?"

"I have no idea, Dad. Mick found her and it looks as if he's claimed her for his own." Delaney took another look before he stepped back from the room, staring at the wet marks on the floor. "I'll mop up, Mom."

"Later, son. Get yourself warmed up."

Graeme watched his son walk away before he approached the bed. "Let's see what we have. Where did he find her?"

"In the meadow, he said. And it was Mick who found her." Moira's hands were working even as she spoke, gently removing the coat and boots and then standing back as Graeme returned with his medical bag.

"Let's see how she is." Graeme finally stood back, the frown he had been wearing replaced by a thoughtful look as the lady began to toss and turn. "We need to calm her, Moira. She has no broken bones that I can tell but there is deep bruising around the ribs and on her face."

Moira nodded. "It looks as if her wrists had been bound too, my dear. And those marks on her neck?"

Graeme sighed. "She was bound. Those appear to be abrasions from ropes. And it looks as if someone tried to choke her. We can't notify her family until she wakes up."

He turned to look at the door before he spoke again. "Was Delaney calling Tom?" Tom Everson was the local police chief and a good friend.

"He said he would report it to Tom. Tom told me earlier that they're overwhelmed with accidents and he needs all his people in town. I suspect he'll have told Delaney if he couldn't make it out today, he'd be out tomorrow. The snow's changed to sleet."

"Then it's a good thing Mick found her."

Moira gathered the clothing and headed for the door, looking back for a moment, a sense of familiarity about their guest wafting through her mind before she shrugged and walked away.

Graeme studied the lady, wondering just who she was before his eyes landed once more on her hands. He reached for her left hand, studying the rings she wore, before a deep sigh was dragged from him. He raised his eyes, not seeing the soft peach walls or cream trim, the deep peach drapes covering the windows. He knew who their guest was, but he wasn't sure how it would go over with Delaney.

Dressed in dry clothes, Delaney peeked out from under the towel he was using to dry his hair, as his father entered the kitchen and walked to the counter, his hand resting on it before he reached for a mug and poured himself a cup of tea. He then turned, leaning against the counter, a hand gripping the edge, his cup in his other hand, as he watched his son closely, his dark brown eyes both thoughtful and concerned.

Delaney moved to drape the towel over the washer in the adjacent laundry room and turned back to his father, stopping at the look on the older man's face.

"Dad?"

Graeme's eyes studied his son. "Delaney? Do you know who she is?"

Delaney shook his head, a frown on his face matching the one on his father's. "I have no idea, Dad. She seems familiar but I didn't get a good look at her face. I didn't want to move her hood and expose any flesh to the weather. Why?"

Graeme didn't speak for a moment. "Refresh my memory. You met your lady on your last trip?"

"I did, Dad. Again. We had met in college and dated before going our separate ways. I've told you that so many times. We fell in love, decided not to wait until we returned home and married about a week before we both had to come home. When we landed here in the area, there was a bomb scare at the airport. We got separated, I was injured when I was knocked down in the rush of people, and I couldn't find her, no matter how much I looked." He watched his father closely. "Why?"

"And what kind of stone did you get for her?"

"A yellow diamond. Very unique setting. I emailed that picture to you." He walked to stand in front of his father. "Dad?" He turned his head to look at the doorway, hearing his mother moving around upstairs before he looked back at his father, seeing a compassionate look on his face. "Dad? What's going on? What aren't you saying?"

"And what was her name again?"

"I've told you. Regan Stuart. Dad?"

Graeme finally sighed, his hand coming up to his son's shoulder before he nodded at the doorway.

"I think you found your lady today, son. Her ring is a match to the picture." His hand tightened on his son's shoulder as Delaney went to move away. "Wait, son. There's something you need to know. Wherever she's been, she was bound at some point. There are abrasions on her wrists. And my examination has led me to believe that someone tried to strangle her."

"Strangle her? Bound?" Delaney broke from his father's grip and ran for the stairs, pausing in the bedroom doorway to stare back down the hallway before he stood staring at the bed. He walked closer, his eyes on her as she lay there, not moving. He moved to where he could see her rings, reaching for her hand, his finger rubbing against the diamond.

His father was right, wasn't he, Lord? This is my Regan, back to me. But how? Where has she been, Lord, and why? Who had her? He dropped to his knees beside the bed, his hand reaching out in a hesitant manner to touch her cheek.

"Why, Lord?" He whispered ever so quietly, his eyes on his bride's face. "Why, Lord? Who did this? Please heal her. Bring her back to me and to her family."

He sighed as his hand reached to stroke her dark red hair, praying she would open the amber eyes he could get lost in. But she lay still, her agitated movements stopped for the moment, barely breathing he thought, and unaware that he was begging her to awaken.

Graeme stood for a moment, his eyes on Regan before he moved to stand beside his son, his hand on the younger's man's head, as he petitioned the heavens to bring this lady back. But when she would awaken, would she still be Delaney's or would she move on and away from his son?

Chapter 2

Delaney hit the bedroom door on the run, tripping over Mick as he did so, his eyes searching for Regan, finding her tossing and turning. His father was there, a hand to her forehead before he reached for his stethoscope. This is one time I'm glad Dad's a physician, Delaney thought, before he stood beside the bed, his hand reaching to touch Regan's face, seeking to calm her. Lord, please? Please? Heal her.

Delaney shoved Mick away from the bed, dropping to his knees beside it, his hands clenching and unclenching before he reached to grasp her left hand. His father stood back for a moment, a frown on his face, before he turned away for a moment, a prayer raising in his heart for the younger couple. He had no idea what she had gone through and a brief thought crossed his mind that she might never be able to tell them.

Delaney's voice murmured close to her ear. What he was saying, he would never be able to tell anyone. Regan's face turned towards him and her eyelids flickered before she sank bank on the pillows, her movements stilling for the moment.

He looked up at his father, catching the frown on his face, and his heart sank.

"Dad?"

Graeme watched his son for a moment before he reached to draw him to his feet.

"We need to talk, son. The middle of the night is not what I would have chosen."

"What about?" His eyes on Regan, he didn't see his father shaking his head before he was drawn from the room and with his father's hand on his back, directed down the stairs to the kitchen.

Graeme just reached to make tea for them, his thoughts bleak, before he slid the mugs onto the table and then sat, his eyes on his hands as he prayed. He had no idea how to tell his son what he had discovered.

"Dad?" Delaney's soft question raised his father's eyes to him. "What's wrong? Something is, I can tell."

Graeme nodded. "There is. Before you came into the room, Regan was awake but she can't talk. Or at least talk above a whisper. I need to get her to the hospital to do imaging on her."

"What are you saying, Dad?"

"That her vocal cords and possibly even her larynx have been damaged. I don't know how severe or if it's even permanent."

Delaney stared at his father, his head beginning to shake. "That can't be. I heard her calling for me. So did Mick."

Graeme watched with compassion as Delaney struggled to compose himself. "She didn't say a word, son. Not a word. She hadn't awakened again when you came in."

Delaney stared at his father. "But I heard her, Dad. I heard her calling to me, asking me to help her." He looked down at Mick, who sat, chin on his leg, watching his master. "Mick heard her too."

Graeme nodded, even as he drew a deep breath. He knew there were cases like what had just happened, but he had never had one himself.

"You two have a connection, son, that I have heard about. I can't explain it. No one can." He raised his mug and sipped at his tea, his eyes steady on his son. He set his mug back down, his hand reaching to rub at the back of his neck. "We won't know for sure what happened to her until she's awake."

"And when will that be, Dad?"

Graeme shook his head. "I'm sorry, son. I don't know. She is rousing but not knowing what happened to her, what she went through, whether she was drugged or not, I can't tell you when. Only the Good Lord knows."

"I just wish He'd tell us, or at least, let her wake up." He shoved away from the table, his mug of tea untouched, and headed for the stairs. He needed to be near Regan, even if she didn't know he was there. Mick paced beside him, close enough that his fur brushed against Delaney's leg.

Delaney sank to a sitting position on the floor, his eyes on Regan's white face, and reached for her hand. He felt her fingers tighten on his and he watched, willing her to awake and know him, but at the same time, afraid for her when she did. He could feel evil around him, around her, and knew that whatever it was she had faced on her own, it was far from over.

His mother paused in the doorway, her eyes watching her son before they shifted to Regan, seeing the younger woman beginning to rouse. Her heart hurt for them even as she moved on past the doorway, a prayer raising for them.

Delaney's head drooped. He had be going without enough sleep, what sleep he had managed to get broken by dreams that caused him to rise and pace, Mick pacing with him. He shifted how he was sitting, his head resting against her pillow, his eyes on their hands. Lord? I don't know how to pray. Not anymore. You know my wishes, dreams, hurts, dear Lord. Please, heal my lady? Bring her back to me.

Delaney slept, not feeling Mick curling up tight to him. He didn't feel as Regan's fingers tightened on his and then her hand slipped from his as she turned to her side, her hand tucked under her cheek. She slept, her sleep undisturbed as she sensed Delaney near to her.

Chapter 3

Rousing a few hours later, Delaney stared around, disoriented for a moment before he felt Mick nudging him. He rose, heading for the bedroom he had been using, knowing it would be a busy day, Sunday and all. He turned for a moment, a frown on his face, before he shook his head and reached for clean clothes and then headed for the shower and for a shave.

He stood on the back deck, the early morning light barely breaking through the darkness. He turned for a moment, his eyes on the back door, before he headed for the garage and the salt and tools he needed for the snow clearing that was ahead. He paused, a frown on his face as he stared down at the footprints that marked the lawn between the garage and the house. His eyes followed the marks to the edge of the trees that lined the back of the property and sighed.

"I hope Tom makes it out today, Mick. He needs to see this." He reached for his phone, sending off a message to the officer, and then headed into the garage. Mick growled, his hackles raising as he threw his body in front of Delaney, sending Delaney backwards through the door.

Delaney stumbled before he righted himself, his eyes on Mick.

"Mick? What are you up to? I need to go in there."

Mick kept blocking Delaney's forward progress into the garage, causing Delaney to step back from the doorway and stare first at his dog and then at the garage. He noted the raised hackles on the dog and heard the low angry growls. His head turned as he heard footsteps behind him.

"Delaney? What is Mick up to?" His father stood there, a puzzled look on his face.

"I have no idea, Dad. He just will not let me go through that door." He turned and pointed. "And then there are those."

"There are what?" Graeme turned and stilled. "That's what he was alerting about this morning. I looked but couldn't see anything. I tried to let him out but he refused to go."

"He did? I never heard him."

"I didn't think you did. I was downstairs and he was growling quite low at the door." Graeme's hand drew Delaney away from the door and back towards the house. "Tom called. He's on his way out. He said he'd bring a tech with him, just in case they were needed."

"Dad? We need to work out here. If Tom's coming, we need to clear the snow and salt."

"No. We're in the house. Now!" He looked up as he heard the sounds of a snowmobile. "That's likely Tom now. He said that's what he'd have to use. The road is impassable at the moment."

"Dad? And you're to work today?"

"No. I talked to the hospital. Any staff that can't get in are told to stay home. They will manage."

Graeme watched as Tom walked towards them before he reached to shake his hand, Delaney following suit. Tom studied them for a moment before he spoke.

“I don’t like the looks on your faces.” Tom looked between the two of them and watched as Delaney turned and pointed towards the garage.

“Mick wouldn’t let me in there just before you came. And then, there are those tracks leading to the back of the yard.”

“Tracks?” Tom was away before they could say anything more.

The two men stood and watched as Tom and the officer with him headed for the garage and then out the back door of it, standing talking before the officer headed towards the footprints and followed them. Tom headed their way, pointing towards the house.

Their boots on the boot tray, jackets on the hooks above, Delaney turned to his father, and then headed for the stairs.

Tom watched him walk away before he turned to Graeme.

“Graeme?”

Graeme just shook his head as he poured them both a coffee and then set a basket of muffins and an assortment of jams on the table before sitting himself.

“I don’t know, Tom. I really don’t know.” He sighed, then bowed his head as his friend prayed for them. When he looked up, his eyes went to the doorway, hearing Delaney walking around overhead. “He’s hurting, Tom, and this time, I can’t make it better for him.”

“No, not this time. You can’t. What can we do?”

“She was awake earlier but couldn’t say much.” Graeme paused, working to control his emotions. “The thing of it is, Tom? She can’t talk.

Not much above a whisper." He repeated the words he had said to his son, watching a stern and sober look cross his friend's face.

Tom sighed, then reached into the backpack he had dropped to the floor beside him, pulling out a pad of paper and his pen.

"Start with what happened yesterday from your viewpoint. Then, I'll need to get Delaney's." He looked up, a closed look on his face. "I will need to see the wounds and abrasions and take photos."

Graeme rose, walking from the room and then returning, handing Tom a card from his camera. "Here. Morag took these for me when I was first assessing Regan. I'll take you up shortly."

Tom finally looked up from his notes. "That's it?" When Graeme nodded, he frowned. "What does Delaney say?"

"He hasn't said much. I think it's been too much of a shock. He's torn." Graeme paused, staring down at the muffin he had torn to bits but not eaten before he sighed, his eyes raising to the doorway as he heard footsteps coming down the stairs and then Delaney appeared in the doorway.

Tom studied him before he pointed to a chair. "Sit, please, Delaney. This is official business at the moment. We need to know how you found her and where and then we need to know what just happened out there."

Delaney nodded, his head dropping forward for a moment as fatigue hit in waves. He felt his eyes closing but didn't feel himself slipping sideways from his chair. He didn't hear the exclamation from his father or Tom as both men reached for him, hauling him to his feet. Arm around him, Graeme motioned with his head to the living room.

"In there, I think, Tom. I've been expecting this." He stood for a moment, assessing his son as he laid on the couch before he turned, a grim look on his face. "Tom, what is going on? Do you know?"

Chapter 4

Tom shook his head. "No, I don't. And I don't like that. I need to talk to them both." He sighed as he heard his phone and pulled it out. "I'm heading out to your garage."

"Tom?"

Tom just shook his head. "I have no idea what's going on. As soon as I can determine that, I'll be back in." He looked down at Delaney. "Will he be awake soon?"

Graeme shrugged, even as he saw Morag motioning for him. "I have no idea, Tom. Come back through when you're done out there."

An hour later, Delaney was on his feet and running for the stairs, his father stopping in the doorway to watch him before he followed him, shaking his head. He had heard no sound, but Delaney seemed to be on a mission.

Delaney hesitated for a moment before he dropped to his knees, his hand reaching for Regan's as she moved restlessly. She stilled under his touch, and her eyes flickered open and closed, finally staying open.

Regan blinked, trying to clear her vision, a frown puckering her forehead. She could hear a low voice talking to her, whispering softly, but she sighed. There was no way it was Delaney. He was dead. They had told her he died in the bomb at the airport. They had been separated and she was pulled into arms and hustled from the site.

She remembered fighting them, trying to get back to Delaney, but she had been shoved into a vehicle and the vehicle had sped off. She didn't remember much after that. She had no idea where she had been or with whom. She just knew she had been kept in a room, on a third floor, she thought. It had been too far to get out of the windows and the door had been locked on the outside. She had heard the snap of a padlock every time it was closed.

She had no idea what day it was or how long she had been gone. She remembered just a day or so ago of trying the door and finding it opening under her hand. She had crept, almost crawled, down the steps to the outside door, finding it opening as well under her hand. She hadn't heard the man who had asked her repeatedly where the man was. She had simply shaken her head, not knowing who he was looking for. She didn't recognize the name.

She had shivered in the dampness of the outdoors, wrapping her jacket tighter around her and pulling her hood forward to protect herself from the snow that had started.

She stumbled as she walked, the snow rising higher and higher in front of her. Her strength had been depleted over the course of the last weeks. She paused for a moment, shrugging deeper into her jacket and then moved forward. She didn't see the fallen branch under the snow until her foot caught on it and she fell forward, a cry torn from her. She laid still, trying to catch her breath, trying to find the energy to rise, to seek for help. I'll just lie here for a moment, she thought. Just a couple of moments. Then I'll get back on my feet and walk forward. There has to be a house around here somewhere. And then her eyes had closed and she had drifted off to sleep.

Her eyes searched the room, not recognizing it. She turned in fright as she heard a man's voice beside her and then realized it was a prayer that she was hearing. She listened closer. A prayer for her. Now who, she wondered, would do that? Not the man who had kept her captive.

She stared at the hand on hers, a frown in place once more, as she studied it. She knew that hand, recognized the wedding band, she thought, but it couldn't be. Delaney was dead. Of that, she had been convinced. She turned her head a bit more and saw the head bent near her and started. She knew that man.

"Delaney?" She tried to talk to him, to call for him, but she could barely get any sound out. But it was enough.

Delaney raised his head, his eyes on Regan, a smile lighting his face as he saw that she was awake.

"Regan! You're awake! Thank God! You're awake." He went to rise but her hand tightened on his and he stopped, watching as her eyes studied him before she sighed.

"Delaney? You're alive? I thought you were dead."

He had to lean in close to hear her words, shock flowing through him as he heard her.

"No, my love. I am alive. Let me go get Dad."

He was on his feet and away before she could stop him. A tear trickled down her temple and she was too fatigued to even raise a hand to wipe it away. She started as she felt a wet tongue on her face and turned, ending up nose to nose with Mick, who gave a low woof of greeting and swiped at her face once more.

Chapter 5

Delaney slid to a stop just outside the door, finding his father standing there, Tom right behind him, and his mother just coming up the stairs.

"Dad? She's awake!" Delaney shot a glance behind him, a frown working across his face.

"She is? Let me take a look and then Tom needs to talk with her." Graeme's hand resting briefly on his son's shoulder before he moved past him and into the room, Morag behind him, the door closing quietly behind them.

"Delaney? How be we have a talk and you can tell me what you found?" Tom's hand on his arm drew Delaney to the reading nook near the top of the stairs. "Sit, son. I know you want back in there but talk to me first."

Delaney dropped heavily into a chair, fatigue weighing him down, his eyes on the closed door, before he turned to Tom.

"What do you need to know, Tom?"

"Walk me through yesterday. What happened?"

Delaney sighed, knowing he didn't have much choice. He began to speak, his attention not totally on Tom, who frowned as he heard the younger man's words.

"And you had no idea who it was?"

Delaney's head shook as he thought back through the day. "No, I didn't. I thought there was something familiar about the person, but I didn't know who it was." His attention turned to Tom. "What was going on in the garage?"

"Someone had broken in. We found evidence of that. Joe's searching through for any evidence. It will be a while before you can get in there." Tom looked up as he heard the door across from them open and watched as Delaney was on his feet and into the room, leaving Tom staring after him.

Delaney paused in the doorway for a moment, his eyes on his father, searching for an answer. Graeme stopped his forward movement and pulled him back out into the hallway, his eyes on his son.

"Dad?" When his father didn't answer, Delaney's gaze shot to the doorway, and his face paled. "Dad?"

"We need to talk, son, before you go in there." He turned Delaney back to the nook and shoved him down into the chair he had just vacated before he sat himself, sending up a prayer.

"Dad? Is she okay?" Delaney shifted in his seat, wanting to run to Regan's side, but wanting to hear what his father had to say.

Tom watched the father and son, a prayer raising up for them and for Regan as well. He waited for Graeme to speak, before his eyes raised to the doorway, seeing Morag standing there.

Graeme finally sighed, knowing he had to be frank with his son. "Delaney? She's asleep again. This time, asleep, not unconscious. She tried hard to tell me what happened but she can't articulate well enough yet to do that." His eyes went to Tom. "It may be a few days yet, Tom, but I'm not sure how well she'll be able to speak. We may need her to write out what happened."

“We can work with that, Graeme, if that’s your concern.”

“It is. Delaney?” Graeme waited until his son looked at him. “Did she say anything to you?”

Delaney’s eyes slid shut and pain flickered across his face. “She did, Dad.” His eyes opened and Graeme drew in a deep breath at the look in them. “She said she thought I was dead. That I had been killed in an explosion at the airport. That’s what she was told.” He was on his feet and moving past his mother to stand for a moment at the bedside before he sat on the edge of it, his hand reaching to touch Regan’s face.

“Regan, what did they do to you? Please, wake up.”

Chapter 6

A week later, Regan moved around the living room in Delaney's home. She was unsure if she should be there, but he had asked and she could not refuse him. She had no idea where they stood now, as a couple. What she had gone through had changed her. That much she knew, not just from her own experience. Having working for her father and being sent to do what he called extractions, finding people and either bringing them to their country's embassy or home with her and one of her siblings, that knowledge had taught her how changed a person could become.

She turned slightly as she heard Mick's nails clicking across the floor towards her before his wet nose nudged at her hand. She rubbed at his ears before she turned to face the room, studying it. Delaney had asked if she would move there to live. She knew she needed to go somewhere, that she couldn't live with his parents, and right now, she wasn't sure she wanted to find her family. She would be smothered, she knew that only too well. She sighed. At some point over the next few days she did need to make contact with them. How she would tell them what she had been through, she had no idea. She paled as she knew she had to confess her marriage. Right now, though, she felt that marriage was up in the air. She did not know if her marriage would survive. It had been too new and strange when the events unfolded.

Delaney stood for a moment, knowing Regan had not heard him, before he sighed. He loved her deeply but he was no longer sure of that love, that Regan shared a love for him. She was changed, that he had to admit to himself. Lord, where do we go? How do we go on? Is it even possible to salvage our love and marriage? Do we need to let each other go? Please, Lord.   Heal my love and keep her safe. Somehow, I just know she's not safe and that I don't like.

Regan looked up as she heard the whisper of Delaney's footsteps approaching her.   She had to brace herself that she didn't jump or didn't move away from him.   Just why she was so afraid of a touch she could not say.

"Regan. Here's your tea." He nodded at the chair she seemed to favour. "Sit, please? Dad says you do need to rest."

She glared at him for a moment before she reached for her mug and turned to the couch, sitting down harder than she meant to, Mick jumping up to lay with a paw and his chin on her leg. She stared down at him.

"Why is he doing this? I don't like dogs that much, you know."

Delaney shook his head, knowing that was not the lady he had met once more, who had adored the pictures he had shown her of his dog, wanting to meet him so badly. "But you see, you do.   You wanted to meet Mick, could hardly wait was how you put it."

Her hand rested on Mick's back for a moment before she looked up at Delaney, her eyes taking in the struggle he was undergoing at that moment. "Delaney? Where do we go from here?"

He had to really listen to catch her words. Her voice was still not more than a whisper and might always be only that loud. She had agreed, reluctantly, to the diagnostic imaging his father had asked for.

Nothing definitive had come from that, other than for swelling and bruising of the area of concern.

He moved to sit beside Mick, his hand resting on his dog before he laid his arm along the back of the couch, watching Regan closely, not seeing her stiffen and shift away from him as she had been. Please, Lord, was his plea. Heal my lady.

"I am really not sure, Regan. First, we need you to heal." He looked down, away from the direct look she was giving him. "I don't want to lose you but if I need to set you free, I will." He looked up at that point, his heart in his eyes, seeing her eyes close and a single tear spill and trickle down her cheek. He watched as Mick's tongue came out to swipe at it before her hand reached to touch the dog's soft head. "God knows where we go. The thing is, I don't think you are done with that man, whoever he is."

She nodded. "I know. I want to go on with my life, but right now, not knowing who he is or what he wanted, I can't. That's not fair to you."

Giving a soft growl of displeasure, Delaney reached to shove Mick to the floor, shifting over until he sat next to Regan, his eyes watchful before he reached carefully to wrap her in his arms, keeping his embrace loose. She started as she turned to search his face before she relaxed back against him, for the first time in weeks, she thought, that she could accept a hug.

Regan finally spoke. "Delaney, how long was it? No one has said. Tom just shook his head when I asked."

"You were gone for four weeks or just a bit longer. I searched for you."

"But you were hurt, weren't you? That's what your Mom said."

"Just bruising and a cut on my forearm. That has healed. What is having difficulty healing is my heart." His arms tightened on her.

She nodded, her gaze on the fire he had lit earlier, watching as the flames flickered. "Delaney, what if I never talk louder than this? How do I go on?"

"God knows, my love." He felt her stiffen at that and knew then her faith had been and was still being sorely tried. His heart raised in prayer for her.

She just shook her head. At the moment, God was far away from her, she thought. He could have kept this from happening.

"What do we do now?" Her heart was heavy, knowing that he would tell her to leave, and she just wasn't sure that's what she wanted to do.

"We take one day at a time, my love. Just one day at a time." He paused, knowing he needed to remind her that he needed to go back to work. "I have to go back to work."

She turned her head, her eyes bleak for a moment before she shuttered them. "I know you do. How long has it been?"

"Too long. I need to start assessing the artifacts that we brought back with us. I have just left them in my workshop. I would like it if you would work with me."

She nodded, before she shoved at his arms and then stood, pacing for a moment. She turned to the window, standing for a moment to stare out at the town street, her eyes watching for what or who, she didn't know.

"I guess." She saw his reflection in the window as he stood behind her. "I have to do something. I can't go back and work for my father when I'm like this. I am not sure that I ever want to do that again."

His hand reached to stroke down her hair that fell in waves and curls halfway down her back. "You've left your hair down. You told me you always wore it in a pony tail or up in a clip. I know you did that, I saw you."

She turned, causing his hand to drop to her shoulder. "I did. I can remember that. I always did." She looked up at him, unsure of how to express herself. "You like it down. I can remember you telling me that. I have forgotten things, that I know, and that frustrates me." Her voice was hoarse at this point and his hand dropped to grasp hers, pulling her to the kitchen, where he pulled out a chair and made her sit.

"Here. Dad sent some of the tea he had for you. Let me make you a cup."

Chapter 7

A week later, Reilly Stuart, one of Regan's three brothers, pulled out a chair in the diner and sat, his eyes on his father, Riordan, who was sitting opposite him. They had come to the town of Whitlock, having been told that Regan might be there. Someone who had seen one of the missing person's poster had phoned in a tip.

"Do you think she's here, Dad?" Reilly didn't want to get his hopes up yet again. They had been told she had been seen in other towns, but nothing had come from those tips.

"This was a credible tip, son. But until we actually see her here, it's still unknown." Riordan looked up with a smile as the waitress set menus in front of them. "Thank you. What is the day's special?"

A short while later, Reilly stared at the young woman standing in the doorway, his hand pausing as he reached for his mug. There was no way that was Regan, he thought. She never wore a long cloth coat, a dress, and boots with a heel, and she certainly never kept her hair down. He tilted his head to study her, his father's attention on his face. Regan always wore jeans, and besides that, always wore her hair up.

"Reilly?" Riordan shifted in his chair to stare behind him. "What is it?"

"That looks like Regan, but it doesn't."

Riordan shifted even more, watching as the young woman greeted the man walking towards her from the cashier, with a hug and acceptance of his kiss on her cheek and then left with him, her hand tight in his. He turned, looking for their waitress.

"Excuse me. That man that just left? He looks familiar but I can't place his name."

"Who? Delaney? That's Delaney Callahan."

"And the young woman? Is that his girlfriend? I know her from somewhere." Reilly was pushing but trying not to be too anxious.

"The lady? That's his wife. Regan, I think he said."

Riordan and Reilly exchanged glances, shock briefly showing.

"His wife? I didn't know he had married." Riordan reached for his wallet. "Can we have our check? I just realized we need to be somewhere out of town in thirty minutes and we have to run."

The waitress stared after them and then shrugged, turning to her next customer, but pausing, not sure if she should warn Delaney or not.

Riordan pocketed his phone as he watched Reilly searching the area. "I have a phone number and an address, but I think we need to make a stop first."

"Dad? Is it Regan?" Reilly was hoping it was.

"I'm not sure, son. We need to speak with the police chief. He's actually my cousin, Tom."

"This is the town you and Mom come to every January? This is Tom's town?"

"It is, Reilly. I just spoke with Tom. He's expecting us."

Tom stood at the open front door to his house, watching as Riordan and Reilly walked towards him.

He had placed a call to Delaney, warning him that Regan needed to be prepared that her father and brother were in town and more than likely had seen them somewhere. Delaney had sighed, stating that he would try and talk to Regan, but she had been adamant that she didn't want to contact her family, not just yet.

"Riordan! This is a surprise. It's not January." Tom reached to shake Riordan's hand before he turned to Reilly. "And which of the boys is this?"

"It's Reilly. Sorry to drop in on you unannounced, but we've come across a situation that we need your help with."

Tom watched the two men as he reached for their jackets, the door closing behind them before he pointed to the kitchen. "In there. I was just finishing off my lunch when you called, Riordan. The coffee pot's on. Help yourself."

Tom watched as Riordan idly turned his mug in his hand, his eyes on his son. Tom sighed to himself. How did he explain what had happened? It wasn't his place to do just that, but he didn't know if Regan would be willing to see her father and brother. He knew she had been putting it off, despite his warning to her that she needed to address that and soon.

"Tom, what do you know about Delaney Callahan?" Riordan's question was not unexpected, Tom thought.

"I know him well. His parents and I are good friends. Why?"

"We saw him today." Riordan paused, his eyes on Reilly, before his heart lifted in prayer. He didn't want to raise his hopes that Regan had finally been found. "The thing of it is, the young lady with him looked like Regan. She's been out of touch for at least six weeks. That is totally unlike her."

Tom nodded, raising his mug to sip at his coffee, trying to frame his thoughts and words in such a way that he would not destroy either Delaney's or Regan's trust in him. "I see." He looked down at his plate. "How be I take you over to meet Delaney? He's the best one to answer any questions you have."

"Tom?" Riordan's question stopped Tom's movements before he shook his head and cleaned up from his meal.

"If you want to follow me, that' s likely best."

Reilly stood outside Delaney's door, watching as Tom knocked and then entered, motioning for the other two men to follow him. He had no idea what they faced, or just why Tom had insisted that they needed to talk to Delaney. But if he knew where his sister was, then that's what they needed to do.

Delaney stood just inside the door, in the entrance to the living room, greeting Tom and then watching the other two men closely. He could see the resemblance between Regan and her father and also with her brother. Regan, he thought, there is just no way we can avoid you meeting them. You need to, not just for your sake. They're hurting and grieving and I'm not even sure they'll understand why you kept away. I'm not sure I even do and we have talked about what you went through, as much as you can remember or if you do remember, what you are willing to share.

Delaney pointed to the living room, excusing himself and then returning with a tray of mugs of coffee.

"Help yourselves, gentlemen." He sat, his eyes on Tom, who nodded. "What can I do for you?"

Riordan and Reilly exchanged a glance, neither wanting to ask the questions but knowing one of them had to.

"We saw you, a while ago, Mr. Callahan, at the diner in town." Riordan began, his eyes on Tom, watching his cousin closely, seeing a shuttered look cross his face.

"That's possible." Delaney waited, not saying anything further.

Riordan sighed to himself. This is not how I wanted to do this, Lord. Guide my words. I don't want to hurt this young man, and if it really is Regan, I certainly don't want to hurt her or alienate her. "We saw you with a young woman. The waitress said her name is Regan." He paused once more to draw in a deep breath, his eyes on his clasped hands, before he raised them to Delaney once more, hope shining in them. "My daughter has been missing for over six weeks. We have searched for her without success, following any and all tips we received. We had a tip that she had been seen in this town. Reilly here thought he saw her with you today."

Delaney watched, compassion on his face. "Call me Delaney, please." He stopped speaking, not quite sure how to continue and looked past the men when he heard the sounds of Regan's low heels tapping on the hardwood floor, heading his way. "Excuse me." He was on his feet and walking towards Regan as she paused out of sight of the living room.

The three men could hear low voices. Riordan frowned as he only heard Delaney's and looked at Tom, catching a look on his face that stopped his gaze on his cousin, a frown in place on his face.

Reilly watched his father closely, a frown on his face as well, before he stood and turned as he heard footsteps coming towards them, two people, he thought. He closed his eyes briefly as he recognized Regan, knowing that it had been her that he had seen earlier. He moved towards her and then halted as she backed away and somewhat behind Delaney, who held her hand in his.

"Mr. Stuart, may I ask that you all sit, please?"

"It's Riordan and Reilly." He sat, his eyes on his daughter, seeing the changes in her, causing his heart to drop. Regan, what happened to you, he thought. Lord, is she okay? There is something different about her and I don't know what or even how to approach her anymore.

Regan paused for a moment, before her eyes caught Tom's nod and then looked up at Delaney, who was watching her, his feelings for her situation in his eyes. He led her to the couch, drawing her down with him, keeping her hand in his.

"Regan?" Reilly's voice was full of hurt, dismay, and questions. He watched her closely before he looked at Delaney and then at Tom.

Tom finally spoke. "Riordan. Reilly. Regan has a story to tell but it will have to be Delaney that tells it or myself to fill in what I can from an active investigation. You see, when Delaney found Regan a couple of weeks, she had had damage done to her throat and that has affected her vocal cords and her larynx. She cannot speak above a whisper or for any length of time."

Riordan's eyes slid closed as pain and disbelief crossed his face before he looked at Regan once more, seeing the proof in her eyes of what he suspected, before he looked at Tom. "Her throat?"

Tom nodded, his eyes on Reilly who was sitting, eyes closed, a look of horror briefly crossing his face. "Her throat? Someone tried to kill her,

38

Riordan. We have no idea who. Regan is not sure even herself who it was. She never saw the man who held her captive for a month."

"Captive? A month?" Riordan's gaze shifted to Regan, finding her watching Delaney, whose eyes were on her brother. "Tom?"

"It's what you think, Riordan. Someone tried to strangle her and for some reason didn't complete the task. Regan is not sure how long it was before she walked away from the building she was held in but it was likely early that same day. Delaney's father, a physician, examined her that afternoon and then had imaging done a week ago."

Riordan's eyes were back on his daughter, finding her this time watching him, a bleak look around her eyes. "Regan? Are you okay now?"

Chapter 8

Watching her father, her brother's shifting on the chair beside him at the edge of her vision, Regan shook her head.

"No, Dad. I'm not." Her voice was barely audible, and Riordan and Reilly had to listen closely. "I'm not sure I ever will be." She looked up at Delaney, who was watching her closely, judging how close to the edge of refusing to talk, to collapse, to walking away once more from her family that she was.

"We have to tell them, love. We can't keep it quiet. They can help search. Tom will let them. And even if he doesn't, they'll search themselves. You know that."

She nodded, tears that she refused to shed sparkling briefly in her eyes before she blinked them away. "Delaney? Will you?"

He nodded, his eyes raising to stare into the distance for a moment, before he looked back at her, his arm coming around her to hold her tight, his hand finding hers. "I will, love. What we talked about is what I'll tell them."

Tom frowned at Delaney's wording, his eyes shifting to Riordan, finding a frown on his face as well.

Riordan spoke, his voice quiet but full of feeling. "Whatever it is, we need to know." He shared a look with Reilly. "Once your mother and the others know, they will want to come here."

Regan began to shake her head, distress on her face. "They can't. They are in too much danger to be around me."

"Regan? What do you mean?" Reilly finally spoke, not sure what she was saying.

Delaney spoke, knowing Regan was at her limit. Any stress drove her ability to articulate to a very low level. "What she means, Reilly, is that her whole family has been threatened. Tom is looking into that but has not been successful in determining who or why."

Tom spoke, his eyes on Regan. "Delaney's correct. I have a detective working on her case but we have no leads. Regan is not even sure where she was kept but it wasn't likely that far from here. Delaney found her in a meadow behind his parents' home. Correction." He smiled as Regan shot him a dark look. "It wasn't Delaney. Not at first. It was Mick." He turned his head as he heard toenails clicking on the floor, and Mick appeared, jumping up to curl up next to Regan, his chin and a paw on her leg.

"Regan? Is that true?" Her father watched her closely, fear in his heart for his oldest daughter. He had had two sons that had been in danger and had prayed the other three would avoid it.

She finally looked up at him, fear on her face, before she nodded, opened her mouth to speak, and then shut it again. Tom rose and headed for the kitchen, returning in a few moments with a mug of tea for her. She whispered her thanks before she looked at Reilly, seeing his worry for her on his face. She looked up at Delaney, who once more nodded.

Delaney began to speak, detailing what Regan had shared.

"We were married, Riordan, about a week before Regan was to come home. I wanted her to tell you about that, but she wanted to do it in person. You never knew we had dated through university for me and college for her. When you asked her to go in on that first trip when she finished college, we had words. We both decided we needed time to think about where our lives were heading and if we were really the one each other wanted to share their lives with. I regret that I lost those years with her. She didn't want to wait until we came home. It was a decision we made together. We had planned on coming here and then heading to you the next day.

"Plans changed. When we landed, there was a bomb threat at the airport. In the panic that ensued, Regan was torn away from me. I was hurt, but more importantly, I lost Regan. I searched for a month for her, every single day. I was out walking with Mick here that day we had that bad snow and ice storm. He found her, snuggling up tight to try and keep her warm, and barked for me to find him. I didn't know it was she that I had found. Dad and Mom sorted out what was wrong with her. It's been about two weeks since that day.

"Regan has been adamant that she doesn't want to bring danger to you or your family, Riordan. She has refused any of my suggestions and hints that we needed to contact you. Tom has respected her decision but did tell her that if after three weeks she was still refusing, he would approach you."

Tom spoke at that point. "That's correct, Riordan. I did give her a deadline. But I don't think she had planned to contact you."

Regan shook her head, and spoke. "I couldn't, Dad. Whoever it is said he'd kill all of you and do it in front of me." She blinked back tears before she buried her face against Delaney, her hand digging into Mick's fur as the dog crawled up on her, his muzzle searching for her face.

"He said what?" Riordan's shocked voice rose and then stilled. He shared a look with Tom and then Reilly. "Who is it?"

Delaney shook his head. "We have no idea. Whoever it is took her from the airport that day and imprisoned her. She was allowed minimal food and water. She has said that every few hours he or another man would appear and ask her where someone was. She was given no name or any details, other than being asked where he was. That last day, she remembers the first man getting very angry when she refused to talk. We think it was at that point he attacked her and then left her for dead. She managed to walk out of the building but she can't tell us how far she walked. It is unclear in her mind exactly what time of day she started off.

"She also said they convinced her that I was killed in an explosion at the airport. That fact helped her to give up. Dad had to struggle to keep her alive the first night we had her back."

Riordan sank back in his chair, his eyes on his daughter, his thoughts racing. "And she can't describe the man at all?"

"She says no. We're not sure if she can't or if she won't. Her terror at times is still intense."

Reilly watched his sister closely, knowing that she was experiencing what the women they had found and brought home had felt. How did he help her, he prayed? Lord? She needs healing and only You can provide that.

"Regan?" Reilly waited until her eyes were on him. "What can we do for you? Other than disappearing again and that is absolutely not an option. You know as well as I do as soon as Mom and Redmond, Rory and Ryanne find out, they will be here."

"They can't! They have to stay away!" Regan was on her feet, running from the room. Delaney heard the back door close, Mick's bark shut off by that sound.

"They won't, will they, Dad?"

Riordan sighed, his eyes on his son. "No, they won't. And she doesn't want them around." He looked back at Delaney, trying to assess him and finding him a hard read, his emotions shuttered. "So, where do we go from here, Delaney? We can't step in and take over. That's not an option. But I can guarantee, her family will not stay away."

Delaney nodded. "We are aware of that. She has expressed that very concern. Tom has been working on some plans, but I don't know that she'll even agree to those."

Riordan sat back, his eyes on his hands for a moment, deep in thought. He vaguely heard the talk around him before he rose, found his jacket, and headed out after his daughter, catching her coat up. He stood for a moment, his hand on the door knob, before he pulled it closed and walked over to Regan, dropping her coat around her shoulders, feeling her move slightly away from him. He sighed. She needed to heal and that was a given, he thought.

"Regan? Your mom will want to see you. I can't not tell her I found you and where." He waited, not seeing her respond. "Whether you want them here or not, whether you like it or not, they will come. You know that."

"I know, Dad. I don't want them hurt. There are things I can't remember." Her voice was hoarse and he was saddened at the damage someone had done to his beautiful vibrant daughter, changing her to someone he didn't recognize.

"We can make some plans, but we need you to work with us. I'm not sure you're ready to do that. We know that only too well from what we do." He paused, his eyes searching the backyard. "Someone's out here, Regan. In the house. Now!" He reached for her arm, shoving her ahead of him into the house, Mick barking loudly and jumping up at him. He slammed the door behind him, turning to stare out the window, not seeing anyone but he knew someone was out there.

The three men slid to a stop in the kitchen before Tom headed for the door and outside, his phone out to call for help. Delaney was at his wife's side, reaching to draw her close. His eyes assessed her, feeling her shaking with terror.

"Riordan, did you touch her?"

Riordan was shocked at the question. "I took her arm to get her into the house. Is that an issue?"

Delaney sighed at he looked down at Regan before he looked up, nodding. "It is. She refuses to let anyone but me touch her. That's been like that since she roused. She can't say why, but Dad talked to a friend of his. That physician suggested that the isolation she was kept in and the terror she was subjected to are part of it." His eyes slid shut as he groaned. "We think part of it is a grieving process she has been working through as well."

Riordan finally nodded, a grim look on his face. "That may well be. I've seen it before in one or two of our cases." He felt his phone vibrating and snuck a peek at it. "It's your Mom, Regan. What do I tell her?"

Regan shook her head, unable to answer. Delaney looked up, concern first on his face, then resignation.

"Tell her to come. And the rest of the family. Talk to Tom about somewhere to stay." He looked down at Regan. "Right now, Regan's past her limit." With that, he swept her into his arms and headed for the bedroom that Regan had liked, leaving Reilly and his father staring after them.

Chapter 9

Turning as he heard footsteps behind, Riordan watched as Delaney paused, his hand rubbing at his cheek before he looked up at Riordan, uncertainty on his face.   Riordan had just finished a conversation with Naomi, hearing her sobs as she realized he had found their daughter. She had turned the phone over to Redmond, who had asked the necessary questions and then stated they were on their way. Ryanne was already working on a place to stay. He would call Rory and Leah and then find Reilly's wife, Aideen, and bring her with them.

Delaney moved past Riordan, reaching for the kettle and filling it before plugging it in. He stood, head down, when he was done, his hands resting on the countertop. This was not how they had planned their day. Regan had agreed to go out with him for lunch and then to head to help with his work. He finally turned, leaning back against the counter, his arms folded across his chest, his eyes on the man he knew was his father-in-law. He was unable to read Riordan to know how he felt.

"Delaney?"   Riordan was not sure how to proceed.   Reilly had headed back into town with Tom, who had not found anything alarming in the yard.

Delaney shook his head. "She's sleeping. She gets overcome and shuts down. Dad said it's to be expected. She is starting to remember more but it always terrorizes her. She doesn't let people near her. She has said she realizes that it's a way she's coping but she has no idea how to get past that."

Riordan nodded. "It can. I have seen it happen. I just never expected it to be one of my own." He sighed. "But then Rory and Leah and Reilly and Aideen had problems, an adventure as they call it."

Delaney stared at him. "Regan mentioned that, but I wasn't sure if she was remembering correctly."

"She is. She hasn't said anything more about the man who held her captive?"

Delaney shrugged. "I'm getting bits and pieces. She wants to remember but the trauma she underwent at the end has buried it all. She won't heal until she does remember, and I'm really not sure I want her to relive what she went through."

"She will need to at some point. They all do." He paused, not sure how to continue.

"When does her mother arrive?"

"She'll be in town by early evening, as well the rest of the family." He turned to stare towards the stairs. "They will all want to see her, and she's just not up to that."

"No, she's not. I know this has not been fair to you. I just couldn't convince her that she needed to talk to you. She's been that scared that you would die."

"I think this is the first time we have been threatened in such a way. I know Rory and Reilly went through some really hard stuff, that almost cost them their lives. I had prayed Regan would escape it." He paused, not quite sure how to phrase the next question.

"Before you ask, Regan is the love of my life. Right now, neither of us is sure where we stand or where we're headed. If I have to, I have told her I will let her go, but God willing, I pray that's not an option."

Riordan shook his head. "No, I don't think you'll have to. But I fear for what you will face." He turned and began to pace, his thoughts racing as to where the young couple would be heading. "Has she described the man, said anything that would lead us to him?"

Delaney shook his head, a bleak look on his face. "Tom has asked and she has told him no, she doesn't remember a lot. She has not even been able to tell us where she was kept. We know it was here somewhere. She has mentioned that she has felt someone watching her the few times we've been out and about town. I haven't seen anything."

Riordan nodded, his hands jammed into his jeans pockets. "That's what I thought. She may never be fully able to remember. We can't catch him if she doesn't." He stopped talking, spinning to stare at Delaney. "No one mentioned if you were able to track her."

"We couldn't, but we did try. The snow and ice covered her tracks. In fact, she was covered with snow when Mick found her. If I hadn't been up there for a walk with him, she wouldn't be here."

Riordan shook for a moment, the terror in losing a daughter in such a manner shocking him. "I didn't know. I hadn't realized that's what you meant." He started to pace again, his mind racing. "How do we do this, Delaney?" He spun, his eyes on the younger man. "How do we bring Regan and her family together?"

Delaney shrugged. "It has to be on her terms and in her timing. She can't see them all together. That's a given. Likely her mother first and then go from there. Who's she closest to in the family?"

"Reilly." Riordan's speech stopped. "And we saw how she reacted today. I have no idea how she will respond to the others. Or even the two wives."

"If she reacted to him like that, then how do we put her into contact with the others? Reilly seemed surprised that she was in a dress and had her hair down. This is unusual for her?"

"It is. It's the total opposite of how we know her. Jeans. T-shirts or sweaters or plaid shirts. Her hair up somehow." Riordan stared at the younger man. "You've changed her."

"No, I didn't. You'll find she's doing this to try and reclaim who she is. She needs a change to do that and this is how she's chosen to do that. I did tell her I liked her hair down but that I was fine with however she wore it. She's remembered part of what I said." He sighed, sadness clouding his face as he blinked back tears. "She can't remember things. Be prepared for that. She tries but fails when she pushes too hard. It's too soon, I think, to when she was captive."

Riordan finally reached for his jacket and slid it on, standing for a moment, his eyes on his keys before he looked up at Delaney. "I left a card on the table in the kitchen with all our numbers on it. Please? Call me later tonight. Let me know how she is. And about tomorrow?"

"We'll see, Riordan. I will not prevent you from seeing her, but she needs the ability to make that decision herself. And right now, I can't guarantee that she'll be willing or even able to meet with any of you."

Delaney stood after he shut the door, his hand resting against his, his head down, unable to think, unable even to formulate a prayer. He finally turned and headed up the stairs, stopping for a moment in the bedroom doorway before he approached the bed, his eyes on Regan as she slept, her movements restless. He sighed. There would be little sleep for him that night, it was a given, he thought.

He turned, heading for the stairs, opening the door to let Mick out and standing for a moment on the back porch, an arm wrapped around one of the round support columns, his eyes on Mick as he romped in the yard, before he turned, freezing as he did so. He had no idea where that large brown envelope had come from, but it was not one of his. He reached for his phone. Tom would be there as soon as he called. Had things just escalated for his lady?

Chapter 10

Regan set her mug down with a thump on the counter the next morning, frustration evident on her face, glaring at Delaney as he stood leaning against the counter beside her, arms crossed, a stern look on his face.

"No! I won't!"

He stopped her with a hand on her arm as she whirled away from him. He watched her tense stance before he spoke.

"You can't run and hide all the time, love. It's not fair to your family. And it's not fair to you. You've had time taken away from your family that you will never recover. You need to start making new memories with them. Just your Mom. That's all we're asking for now. See your Mom. She needs that. She's been grieving for you and now that you're here and she can't see you, she doesn't understand. She's grieving that."

She had turned to face him as he spoke, dismay, fear, and then acceptance flickering across her face. She moved into his space, accepting the hug he offered, her hands clutching at his shirt, tremors running through her.

"How do I do this, Delaney? How do I meet with them? You told me about the envelope you found, just not what was in it. If it's a threat against them, how do I see them?"

"They know the risks and accept them. It's you they're worried about. I talked to your Dad last night, just to let him know you were okay for now. He's working to try and find out what happened, but he needs to talk to you at some point. I know you're remembering more and more. Write down what you remember. Hand that to him. He can work with that. He has asked for that, in fact."

She finally nodded, leaning back to look up at him. Her voice had hoarsened with her emotions. "I can do that. When do we meet? And where? Not here, please, Delaney."

"Tom suggested his place or my parents have offered to have us there. Dad would like to be there when you meet with your family, not only as family but as your physician for now."

She finally nodded, spinning to walk away, her heels clicking on the floor, Mick's nails clicking in time with them, his face turned up to watch the lady he adored. Delaney watched before he shook his head, his hand shaking slightly as he raised his mug before it thumped back on the counter. He ran his hands through his hair, trying to come up with a plan that wouldn't hurt Regan anymore than she had been hurt and coming up with a complete blank. It's up to You, Lord. You'll have to be the one who works this out. I know the storm she's in will only get worse. I can feel the fury of it building around us. Keep my lady safe, dear Lord. Heal her.

He walked to his office, not seeing Regan, but knowing she had likely found her comfort spot in the conservatory, surrounded by the plants, Mick tight to her side despite her protests. He sank into his black leather chair, his eyes on the doorway, wanting to go to her, but knowing he needed to let her have time to absorb their discussion. He sighed as he looked down at his desktop. He needed to be working but she had priority. He picked up his phone, his thumb running up and down the side of it before it slid across the face of it, awakening it. He searched for Riordan's number but instead called his father, asking for his advice.   He ended the call, knowing his parents would be willing to have the family meet there.   His father had suggested it even before he asked, telling him to send the whole family there. He and Regan could come in at any time and leave at any time.

He flipped the phone over and over in his hand before he finally searched for Riordan's number and called him,

"Delaney? You have news?" He could hear the desperate hope in Riordan's voice and his eyes slid shut. He could only imagine how he felt.

"I do. Take your whole family to this address. It's my parents'. They want you to come there." He heard Riordan as he asked for a pen and paper and then heard his voice back on the line. "They are expecting you there any time. Regan has agreed to come and meet her mother, but I'm not guaranteeing even that at this point. Nothing is certain with her, not anymore. Your family needs to understand that. That she is not the daughter or sister that she was. This has changed that. She will never be back to that."

"We understand, Delaney. We see it too often, given our line of work." Riordan's voice died away before he spoke again. "We'll be there. I have warned them all what to expect and how to act with her. They don't totally understand, so we'll need to be prepared to take steps if necessary. Reilly has stressed this as well."

"We'll see you shortly, then. Thank you for understanding." Delaney's voice broke as he heard Riordan's whispered thanks to him and his assurance that he was a member of their family now.

He looked up at that point to see Regan standing hesitantly in the doorway.   He rose, his hands reaching for hers, standing staring down at her, his heart breaking for her and for her family, and then raising in prayer for them all.

"Are you sure, Regan?" At her nod, he gave a small smile. "Dad asked we meet at their place. If that's okay with you?"

She sighed. "I'm not sure this is a good idea, though." Her voice had hoarsened overnight and he knew it was part of the stress she was under. "All of them?"

"All of them. But your Dad and Reilly have stressed to them what needs to happen and how you can and will react under stress. Your Dad is in shock, I think, not having expected this type of situation to affect one of his own."

"No, we never expected this. That envelope, Delaney? Was it a threat?"

He wrapped her in his arms and his head came down on hers. "It was, but it was so vague Tom doesn't know quite what to make of it."

"Mick has to come. I need him." She dropped to her knees to wrap him into a tight hug. Mick stood still, knowing that was what he needed to do.

"He can. There's no question about that." He held out a hand to help her stand, taking in the navy sweater she had on, the embroidered denim skirt, and the colourful scarf she had knotted around her neck. "Do you need to take anything with you?"

She shook her head. "Just you and Mick."

Delaney paused inside the kitchen door at his parents, his arm around Regan as she leaned into him. He could hear muted voices and knew her family was there. He heard his father's footsteps and watched as he entered the kitchen, a tray in his hands that he set down quickly and then walked towards his son, his eyes on Regan.

"Regan?" His voice startled her and she jumped even as her eyes raised to him. "Are you sure about this?"

She shook her head. "I'm not." The two men had to listen closely to hear her words. "But it has to be done, doesn't it? Did you talk to them? Tell them what to expect? Tell them what I can and can't do?"

"We have, both your father and I. Reilly contributed to the discussion and I must say he can be very forceful with his words."

She gave a small smile. "He can. He knows me best. Or at least he did. Now, none of them know the me I've become. Only Delaney, you two and Tom do. I hate that, Graeme. I really hate that."

She looked around him as she heard other footsteps, ones she recognized, even as she moved back towards Delaney, finding his arms around her, holding on to her, as her mother entered the room, unaware that her daughter was there.

Naomi Stuart came to an abrupt halt, her eyes widening with shock as she recognized Regan before she set down the plate she had been holding and moved towards Delaney and Regan, coming to a halt as she watched Regan move around Delaney to stand behind him, where she could watch her mother from safety.

"Regan?"

Regan heard the puzzlement in her mother's voice and then looked around Delaney at her, not moving towards her. "Mom? You shouldn't have come."

Naomi was shocked at the low tone of her daughter's voice, even though she had been warned.

She saw the change in her, not liking it, but not sure how to address it. "Regan?"

Regan looked at Naomi and then leaned into Delaney's back. He could hear her whispering that this had been a mistake, she shouldn't have come, before he turned, sweeping her into his arms, blocking her view of the room before he moved her away from the kitchen, through a second door and to the sunroom, seating himself and drawing her down with him, his arms tight around her.

"It's too much for you, love. We'll stay here. Let you get your bearings. Mom and Dad will keep them away from here. You know that."

She nodded, but he could feel the shaking getting worse and his heart broke even as he raised prayers for his love.

"I remember something, Delaney, and I don't know how to tell them."

"Tell who? Your family?"

She nodded. "It has to do with one of the extractions. One that didn't go well. It chewed Rory and I up and spit us out. We didn't get there in time to get the lady out. I have felt watched since then, but I don't know who by." Her voice was fading as she finished.

"Okay, so we tell your father and Tom and they look into it. You never said a word to your father, did you?"

She shook her head, her hand tightening on his arm. "No. I thought I was imagining things at first, but then I had nothing definite I could tell him about. Even now, I don't know the names."

Delaney had raised his eyes, hearing soft footsteps and seeing Riordan standing just outside the door, his eyes fastened on Regan before they raised to Delaney and he nodded before walking away.

"Your Dad was just here. He heard you."

Regan drew a deep breath. "Then, he just signed their death warrants, didn't he?"

Chapter 11

Later that morning, Delaney stood in his father's office, his eyes on Riordan who sat on the corner of the desk, his own father seated in his chair. He knew her brothers were behind him, low voices sounding from there. He listened as Riordan made suggestions, his comments being echoed by Rory, he thought. No, that was Redmond. He knew Regan was with his mother and hers. The other ladies, he wasn't quite sure where they had ended up.

He finally shook his head, his eyes finding his father's and then turning, walked away, leaving a stunned silence behind him.

"Did he really just do that?" Redmond walked to the door, watching as Delaney walked up the stairs to find Regan.

"We warned you, Redmond. We told you how protective he is of Regan." Riordan stood, his eyes on his sons. "Now, you may well not get a chance to see her today. He may well decide she's had enough and take her home. That is his right as a husband. Reilly, Rory, you understand that. What you three don't understand is how she is right now. She is very fragile and scared."

Graeme nodded, adding his voice to the mix. "Your father's correct. She is very fragile. She is not the sister you had. She never will be again. You have to understand and accept that. If you can't, then she will not be around you. That much she has told me."

Riordan was nodding as he listened. "He's right, boys. We have to work with both Delaney and Regan. He's the judge of how and when. Not us.

Regan's not able to make those decisions for herself right at the moment." His voice dropped off as he fought to control his emotions. "Delaney told me earlier today that it had to do with one of our trips. She wasn't clear enough for him to be able to tell me but he felt it was that last one you and she went on, Rory."

Rory paused, his thoughts returning to that trip, and his eyes closed. "There was always something about that one, Dad, and none of us can figure it out. Why?"

Riordan shrugged. "We're working on that, but you know we don't have all the facts."

They all spun as they heard a sudden scream. Graeme was on his feet, running for the stairs, recognizing Regan's voice and wondering that it was so loud. Riordan was right behind him, her brothers staring at one another before they too ran.

Graeme slid to a halt inside the library on the second floor, his eyes on Morag who was moving towards him, pointing to the end of the room. He followed her and found Delaney on the floor, sitting, Regan wrapped in his arms, his head down on hers, her arms tight around his neck, Mick trying his best to reach her face. Graeme knelt, his hand on Regan's back, feeling the violent shaking rocking her body.

"Delaney? What happened?"

Delaney shook his head, not looking up. His father had trouble hearing him.

"I don't know. I came in as she was talking with her mother. Then, she's down at this end of the room and you heard her. I don't know how she managed to scream that loud."

"Will she let me look at her?" He tilted his head. "Regan? Can you look at me?"

She didn't move for a moment, then lifted her head, her eyes on him, a tortured look in them. "He's been here, Graeme. Somehow he's been in your house." Her hand shaking as she lifted it and pointed towards the bookshelves at the other end of the room. "There's a photo there. It wasn't here the other day Delaney and I were up here."

Graeme spun on his knee, then rose, striding rapidly to the bookshelves, his eyes searching before his hand reached for the photo she meant. He stared at it, not recognizing anything about it. Riordan stood at his elbow and Graeme heard the muttered exclamation.

"You know this place?"

"I do. It's a place I prayed we would never see again." He looked up at Rory as he approached. "She was right, Rory. It's that place you went into. How does that relate to this, though?"

"I have no idea, Dad." Rory turned to watch Regan, his eyes sorrowful as he did so. "Who is doing this, Dad? I thought that trip was legit, even though we failed to bring out the lady in time."

"I thought so too, son." He shared a look with Graeme, who had also turned to watch Regan. "Graeme? You have thoughts?"

"I don't know your family and don't quite know what you do for a living, but Regan has said some things. Things I don't think she has ever expressed to you." He sighed, knowing the burden of telling Riordan that Regan would no longer be part of his team. "She is adamant that she won't travel . That she will no longer help you bring people out to safety. She was trying to find the words to tell you that when she took that leave of absence and went away. Delaney hasn't said a lot of what their talks were about that month before they came home, but he

61

has said some of them were pretty intense with her descriptions of what she had to do." He turned and walked from the room, searching before he headed down the stairs and to his office. Tom would come, he knew, but for a moment, he was almost afraid to call him. Was someone in town working with whoever it was?

Tom stood for a moment, his eyes on the photo, before he looked up at Riordan. "You know this place?"

"Unfortunately, I do. We were asked to go in and bring out a young woman. Rory and Regan went in as I felt they were the best two. You know how we work. Always two go in. And we assess before and during that time the danger they are in. This time, the young lady was dead before they even got to her. They escorted her body home to her family. Neither one will give more than the bare facts, but I feel something happened to one of them. Something was said, they saw something, they were threatened. I have no idea what. And I think that someone was Regan. She won't talk about that time."

"She needs to. None of you can get her to do that? Not even Reilly, who you say is closest to her?"

"None of us can. Not even Leah or Aideen. Delaney I think is the one is reaching through to her. He doesn't push her, but lets her talk, asks questions."

"That is Delaney, for sure. He always has been that way. His patience is what makes him good as an archeologist. Regan has been helping him when she's able to."

"That's what I understand." Riordan turned as he heard footsteps and Delaney appeared in the room. "Delaney?"

"Dad's given her a sedative and she's asleep."
He gave a harsh laugh. "As asleep as she ever is."

63

Chapter 12

Regan turned from the window she had been staring out of a few days later as she saw Rory's reflection appear behind her. She wrapped her arms around herself as she studied her brother. She knew he was content and happy in the life he was making with Leah and her bed and breakfast. She also knew he had regretted the danger Leah had been under, even though it had not come from him.

Rory stopped, his head tilted to watch his sister. They had worked well as a team, reading each other's minds without words being necessary. But that was work. He had never been as close to her as he would have liked to have been. He was just older than her, Redmond the oldest in the family, Ryanne the youngest.

"Regan?"

She just shook her head. Her screaming the few days previous had hoarsened her voice to the point that it was difficult to understand her words. Graeme had bluntly told her not to talk, unless she had to, and had handed her a pad and pen, pointing to them and telling her to use them. He couldn't guarantee what damage she had done that would never be healed.

"Rory? What happened to us that time?" She moved past him to drop onto the couch, tucking her legs up under her skirt and then reaching for a pillow to hug to herself, her eyes on her brother.

Rory dropped down beside her, keeping enough distance that she wouldn't feel threatened. He hated that. He always felt that Regan gave the best hugs in the family, her touch soothing. He had told her she would make a great mother and she had laughed at him, saying it was unlikely ever to happen. She was not marrying anyone, ever.

"I don't know. I always feel like we were set up, but Dad had researched it thoroughly as had the team. He would not have had us go in otherwise. I think we were delayed somehow getting the information we need. Dad mentioned there was a bit of a delay, which is not unusual." He paused, his eyes on his sister. "You feel this is related to what you went through?"

She nodded, swallowing hard as she remembered the terror she felt. "I do. I think whoever it was arranged that is after Dad. I don't know why." Her voice was low enough that Rory had to strain to listen to her. She reached beside her for the pad of paper sitting here. "Here. Can you look up these names without telling Dad or Tom? They'll want to know why if we do."

"You think these names are involved in that?" He read through them, his face paling as he read the name at the very bottom. "This one?"

She nodded. "We need to. We have to look at everyone." She looked around, not seeing Delaney and knowing he was in his workshop and had been since early morning, trying to work through what he had in there. "I can't tell Delaney. It would break his heart."

"It would. I'll look into these. Leah and I have to head back today. She needs to be at the bed and breakfast." He paused, his eyes on his hands twisting the paper before he looked up. "You and Delaney are welcome to come and stay any time. It might help to get away from here."

She shook her head, a sigh wrenched from deep within. "I don't think so. Leah gave me your news, the news you haven't yet shared with Mom and Dad. I won't put you at risk."

Rory grinned for a moment. "No, we haven't shared that with them. Leah thought you needed some good news."

"Thank you. Now, you need to get on the road. A storm is moving in. They can get nasty along this shore."

Rory laughed, pausing for a moment, his eyes on his sister before he rose and told her he'd be in touch and that he loved her. She watched him walk away, and heard the door close behind him before she was on her feet to rush and lock it after him. She didn't feel safe that day and she had no idea why. The discovery of the photo at Graeme's had disturbed her more than she would admit.

Delaney stood watching her, startling her when she turned.

"Regan?"

"It's okay. Rory just left." She walked past him, as he sighed and looked up.

She's doing it again, isn't she, Lord? Trying to work it out on her own. He walked after her, stopping her movement with a hand on her arm. She looked up at him, a frown on her face.

"Who just left?"

"Rory. Why?"

Delaney shook his head even as he moved past her. Tom had called, asking if Regan had told him about the letter she had received. When he said no, Tom had muttered away and told him he needed to talk to her, right then. She had been threatened, he was informed, not her family. Regan. What would it take to make her talk?

She watched him before she walked to the table and sat, her hands folded in front of her, trying to compose herself but not quite succeeding. She jumped as a mug appeared in front of her and then Delaney sat beside her.

"What happened, Regan?"

"Tom called you. He threatened to if I didn't talk to you. He didn't give me a chance."

"No, he didn't. He's that concerned. He said you had received a letter."

"I did. It came this morning when he was here about the other day. Then Rory showed up." She rubbed at Mick's head as his chin rested on her leg. "The letter was brutal."

"Tom read it to me." Delaney watched her face closely. "What do we do now, Regan? If you can't remember anything more, how do we find him? And how do we keep you safe?"

She shrugged, rising to dump out her tea before she turned to him. "You need to be working. I'll come keep you company if that makes you any happier." She walked away from him, heading for her coat and the outdoors, Mick pacing beside her.

Chapter 13

Standing back to study the windows of the house, Redmond's fear grew within him two days later. Neither Delaney or Regan were answering and he knew they were home. He had checked the garage when no one answered at his first knock, and there were vehicles in it. He stepped from the porch, heading for the back of the house as quickly as he could, his eyes in constant movement. Where are they, Lord? They should be here. Delaney told me last night they weren't planning on going anywhere.

He tapped at the kitchen door, stepping back to study the back of the house. He couldn't hear Mick and that concerned him. His hand reached for the door knob at it turned and the door slowly opened.

He stepped through, his eyes on Delaney, shock at his appearance vibrating through him. He took in the white face, the unshaven look, the lines that had deepened since he had last saw him, the dark circles under his eyes. He could tell Delaney had not been sleeping and he was sure he had lost weight.

"Delaney?"

Delaney blinked at Redmond, peering through bleary eyes at him before he turned and headed for the counter, reaching for the coffee pot before he set it back down. He leaned on the counter, his hands flat, his head hanging down before he felt Redmond's hand on his arm, drawing him to a chair and shoving him down. Redmond set a mug in front of Delaney before he turned to let Mick out, standing outside watching the dog search the yard. He could see

Mick's hackles raised and knew someone had been there.

Mick ran by him back into the house and Redmond watched as the dog disappeared down the hallway. He knew Mick was heading for Regan, just how he could tell, he didn't know. He slid out of his jacket, dropping it over a chair back before he sat, his eyes on Delaney, compassion filling him.

Delaney raised his head, his eyes on the kitchen doorway, before he spoke.

"Redmond? What are you doing here? I thought you were heading out of town."

Redmond simply shook his head. "No, Reilly went to the conference instead. Dad wanted me here. He wanted me to do some research for you."

"He did?" Delaney's head dropped back down as fatigue hit.

"Where's Regan?"

Delaney gave a laugh. "Regan? She's still likely pacing somewhere. I can't get her to settle down."

"You can't? How much sleep have you two had?"

Delaney just shook his head, fatigue continuing to weigh his body down. "In the last three days? Likely none to little. Regan just won't settle down. She's pacing, silent, withdrawn. I have never seen her like this."

"What happened?" Redmond knew his sister, or thought he did. He felt sure something had arisen since he had last seen her to cause this.

Delaney pulled out his phone, searched for a photo, and silently handed it over to Redmond. Redmond watched him for a moment, seeing the pain and fear, no, terror, he thought, and worry he was trying hard to hide.

Redmond's eyes dropped to the phone and he drew in a sharp breath, before looking up at Delaney, finding the younger man with his head down on his arms, his shoulders shaking.

"Delaney? Does she know this?"

"She does. Tom was here when she got it. He called me before she had a chance to tell me. Rory had been here right after Tom left."

"She couldn't have said anything to him, or he would never have left."

"She didn't. She hasn't been able to tell us anything more about where she was held. I know it was close to here. She can't have walked that far." Delaney sat back, scrubbing the heels on his hands at his eyes before rubbing them down his face. "She just didn't have the strength to do that." He rose, hearing a sound from the conservatory and heading towards Regan, Redmond at his heels.

Regan stood for a moment in the centre of the room, her arms wrapped around herself, before she began to turn in a circle, her hands coming up to rub at her temples. She saw Delaney and stopped, before moving towards him, into his arms, her arms around him.

"Delaney? Where is he? He's been here, hasn't he?"

"Who has, love?" Delaney just stood, holding her, trying to bring comfort, feeling Mick standing up at him, trying to reach Regan.

"That monster." She turned a bit and frowned. "Redmond? Why are you here? You're not supposed to be, are you? Don't tell me. Dad sent you."

"Reilly went in my place. Dad asked that I stay and do some research. Are you able to talk with me and make sense?" A sparkle of mischief peeked out of his eyes as he watched his sister, shocked at the change in her in just a few days. "You need to sleep, Regan."

"I can't, Redmond. I hear him when I'm sleeping. I hear the music and voices that he played when he wasn't there."

Redmond held up a hand, his eyes meeting Delaney's. "Wait a moment, Regan. You never told us that."

"I didn't? I thought I had. That's what he did. He kept bright lights on, too. I couldn't sleep, and if I slept, I had nightmares. Can you find him and stop him? Please, Redmond? I won't ask anything else of you for the rest of my life if you can."

Redmond began to laugh, drawing a frown from Delaney. "It's okay, Delaney. She promises that all the time. Always has. Probably always will." He sobered as he took in how his sister looked, devastated at the change in her. "I'm trying, sis. We need you to help us, though."

She nodded, her head going down against Delaney as fatigue washed through her. "His name is Dexter or Baxter. Something like that. I wasn't supposed to hear it but the other man called him that. That man's name was…". Her voice dropped away. "His name was Eric." She looked up at Delaney, catching the look in his eyes that warmed her. "I did good, huh?"

Delaney hugged her tight. "You did. You remembered. I knew you would." He didn't tell her that he knew the men, quite well in fact. How they fit into his life and hers, he had no idea. Not yet. But he knew Tom would look into it. Then, he paused.

He couldn't go to Tom. Eric was his brother and that wouldn't do. He exchanged a look with Redmond, who nodded, his phone out to take notes.

Chapter 14

Watching as Regan finally slept, stretched out on the inflatable air mattress on the conservatory floor, Delaney sighed. This is not how he pictured his life. He needed to find those men and he was not sure that he could. His eyes slid shut as his head dropped back against the chair he had pulled close to the mattress and he slept. Mick lay beside Regan, his eyes shifting between his two humans, before his head raised and then he was on his feet, moving towards where he heard Redmond.

Redmond looked up from the papers he had spread out on the kitchen table, his eyes on Mick as the dog approached him, reaching out to absentmindedly rub at the dog's ears. He had been in touch with his father and that call had not gone well. His father had been dismayed, to put it lightly, that his cousin, Eric, was involved.

Mick turned away from Redmond, heading to the front door, his hackles raising as he gave low growl. Redmond rose, following on silent feet, standing to the side to watch through the window as the man approached the door, stopping just short before he turned and walked away. That was strange, Redmond thought, pulling out his phone and catching a photo of the man as he turned back to the house.

Delaney stood watching for a moment. "Who was it, Redmond?"

Redmond shrugged. "I'm sorry. I have no idea. But I took this photo." He handed Delaney his phone.

Delaney sighed as he looked down at it. "That's Eric, Tom's brother, cousin to your father, and cousin to you two."

"He was here?" Redmond turned back to the door, watching closely. "That was nervy, I must say."

"He is probably trying to find out if Regan has remembered anything. Tom can't say, so this is the only way he would know." Delaney turned from the door, heading for the kitchen, opening the fridge and staring into it before he closed it and then opened the freezer compartment before he closed that as well, turning to open and close cupboards.

Redmond watched, a prayer raising for his brother-in-law and sister, for healing and protection, before he grinned.

"Can't find what you're looking for?"

Delaney turned his head, a frown on his face, before he replied. "I'm not sure what I'm looking for, to tell you the truth. I don't think I'll find whatever it is in the kitchen."

Redmond stood beside him for a moment before he turned Delaney to the table once more. "Sit, Delaney. I'll make you something to eat. I suspect you haven't eaten either."

Delaney slumped in his chair, a total picture of worry and dejection. He felt at this point even God had abandoned him. "No, I haven't. At least, I don't think I did. Check the dishwasher. If it's empty then I haven't. And I can't get Regan to eat either." His head raised as he heard a sound at the door and he rose and headed towards it, finding his parents stepping inside.

His mother reached to hug him and then headed for the kitchen, basket in her hands that

Redmond reached to take from her. She looked back over her shoulder before she turned back to him.

"I know these two are not eating. Here, plug that crockpot in. It has soup that should be good for them."

Redmond inhaled and grinned. "This smells so good. I might not let them have any."

Morag stared at him for a moment before breaking out into laughter. "I think you'll have to. It's Delaney's favourite. Where is Regan?"

"Asleep in the conservatory. Delaney set up an air mattress for her." Redmond stopped, a bleak look on his face. "She hasn't slept in days, he said. She admitted to us today that she couldn't sleep when she was captive and why." He looked up as he heard the other men approaching. "Delaney?"

Delaney nodded. "Dad knows. Mom, I need to tell you something in confidence. Please don't let Regan know you are aware. She has named Baxter and Eric as the ones who held her."

"Baxter? Now, that I can see. Eric? As in Tom's brother?" At his nod, she frowned and then nodded herself. "Yes, I can see that. He hides what he does but I know for a fact he's working and living on the other side of the line."

"You never said anything, Morag." Graeme reached for the kettle to fill it.

"No, I couldn't. But now I have to. The one who told me is no longer alive and it was a commitment to them not to tell, unless I absolutely had to, while they were alive." Morag walked away, looking for Regan, leaving the men staring after her.

"Did she really just say that, Dad?"

"She did, son. And she's right. We can't go to Tom with this. It's a conflict of interest for him now. But how do we not tell him?"

Redmond spoke from where he was leaning a shoulder agains the wall. "I'll talk to Dad or Rory and get them looking into it. It's not as close a relationship with Dad. Let him find what he can and then we can go to Tom." He looked down at the fingers he was rubbing together. "It's going to hurt, no matter how we do it."

Delaney walked towards Regan, hearing her voice, and knowing that she was awake again. He sighed. Lord, I could use Your help. I need to get Regan to sleep and to relax, and it isn't happening. I need her to trust You for that and she's shutting me out. Touch her, Lord.

He watched as Regan moved away from Morag, her eyes searching. Seeing him, she almost ran to throw herself at him.

"He's been in here, Delaney. I can feel him. He's left something."

"We'll look and find it. Where do you think?"

"In here. Now, he's taken my sanctuary from me." She bit out the words in anger, the first emotion he had seen other than terror. She spun away from him, to search the book shelves and then through the furniture, finally stopping, her hand frozen on a drawer pull as she stared down at it. "I was right. Here. In this drawer. Lord, why? Why did You let him in here? I need somewhere on the main floor I can feel safe and I don't feel safe here anymore."

Delaney stood behind her, his hands opening and closing before he reached to wrap her in a hug, his head tilted to look down in the drawer, breathing in sharply as he saw a photo from their wedding.

"He was there. I didn't see him. How did he know?"

77

Chapter 15

Riordan looked up at Rory as he paused beside his desk, not liking the look on his son's face. He threw down his pen as he leaned back in his chair, watching as Rory paced.

"Rory? You weren't to be in today. Is Leah with you?"

Rory turned to his father, shaking his head. "No, she's not. This is a quick trip, Dad. Redmond called. He said Regan named the two men."

Riordan leaned forward, his arms on his desk, an interested look on his face. "She did? I didn't think she had remembered that." He watched as Rory struggled with what he needed to say. "Is it that bad, son?"

Rory sank into a chair, his eyes on his father even as he nodded. "It is, Dad. It really it. First, she said that music or voices were played when the men weren't there and a bright light was on at all times. She indicated she barely slept and always dreamed if she did." He drew in a deep breath. "But that's not what has me concerned. It is who she has named. Delaney recognized both names."

"And they would be." Riordan reached for the folder Rory handed him, frowning as Rory didn't let go of it. "Rory?"

"It is bad, Dad. She saw one was named Baxter. Delaney knows him. He's a teacher at the high school and taught Delaney." He swallowed hard. "The other one is Eric."

"Eric?" Riordan paused, his hand coming to rub at his cheek before he rested his chin on his clasped hands, elbows on the desk. "As in my cousin?"

Rory nodded. "That would be the one."

Riordan stared at the folder for a moment. "And I gather you have brought me everything you can find on the two." He looked up. "We can't go to Tom. Not yet."

"That's what Redmond says, but how do we do this without letting him know?"

"We'll figure it out. Now, about Regan. How is she?"

Rory just shook his head. "Delaney told Redmond she hadn't slept in three days and he hadn't either. She did sleep for a while but not enough to help. She also found a photo from their wedding in a drawer. And it's not one they took or had taken."

"He was that close to them, even then? So this has been planned for a while. Who would they be looking for?" He scanned the material in the folder. "How much have we looked into Delaney?"

"A thorough search, Dad, as much as we would anyone we were hiring. He's clear and so are his parents. He's not going to be going to any sites . He told Redmond he'll be teaching now, which helps, but doesn't help."

Riordan was on his feet, reaching for his jacket. "Do you have time to come with me to Regan?"

"Not today, Dad. Leah has a function she has to be at and I promised her I would go with her. I'm needing to get back on the road." He walked out to the vehicles with his father, praying for him and for his sister and Delaney. This was hitting too close to home once more.

Riordan stood outside Delaney's home, studying it much as Redmond had done earlier that day before he shook his head. Lord, I have no idea where this journey is taking us, other than through a storm, and I can feel the fury of that storm building around my daughter. I can't stop it. I can't take her out of it. It's not my place. Not , much as I want to. All I can do is walk through it with them. Lord, please calm the storm, the winds. Bring healing to our Regan. He looked around, feeling uncomfortable and not sure why. He turned back to the steps and found Graeme standing there, mugs of coffee in his hand.

"Riordan. I thought you'd be around. Did Naomi come with you?"

"No, she's out of town with Ryanne for a couple of days. Bonding time, she said." Riordan took the mug with a quiet word of thanks before nodding towards the house. "What's the situation like in there?"

Graeme shrugged before he sipped at his coffee. "About the same. Delaney's worn out. He has to start teaching in another four weeks and I'm not sure he's going to be able to. This had taken a lot from him. It's taking a lot from Regan as well. Morag has gotten her to finally go to bed, but it has to be on the main floor. She's refusing to climb the stairs."

"I can understand that. I've seen it before." Riordan looked up as he felt someone else there. "Delaney? Where's your coat?"

Delaney shrugged, not really caring that it was still a cold day. "Inside. Dad, Mom's looking for you. She said something about a meeting you had to be at."

Graeme nodded, even as he handed his mug to his son. "She's right. I'm off. I'll be back later."

Riordan walked towards the conservatory, not hearing any voices. He stopped in the doorway, watching closely as Regan slept before he looked at Morag.

"She's sleeping?"

"She is. Delaney finally agreed to let his father give her a sedative. He had been holding off on that as she was drugged when she was held captive."

Delaney spoke from behind him. "That's right. She fought me on that. But I had no choice. She can't heal if she doesn't sleep."

"Nor can you." Riordan hesitated before he asked. "Do you have a few minutes, Delaney? I would like to talk with you about what you two boys discovered this morning."

Delaney shot him a quick look at being called a boy, and then shook his head at his mother, who was laughing softly. "I do. Then, I need to crash. I can hardly keep my eyes open."

"I understand that, Delaney. Here. Redmond has his paperwork in the kitchen, doesn't he?"

"He does. And it looks as if you had more to add to it."

"I do. Rory was busy. He's still searching but he has come up with a lot, including an address I need to ask you about."

"And that would be close to here? About a mile from Mom and Dad's?"

"That close? Then, yes it would be." Riordan dropped the folder on the table and reached for his mug, knowing he would need something to keep him going. He still had to call Naomi and that was a call he was not looking forward to.

"What did Rory find, Dad?"

"An address for one thing. It's outside of town, isn't that correct, Delaney?"

"It is and that means we have to call in another police force." Delaney's head dropped to the arms he had folded on the table. "This just gets better and better, doesn't it?"

"It may help, Delaney. I understand your concern with who she has named. She doesn't know the history or the connection to our family. I can't understand what they want."

"Regan keeps saying they were looking for a man. She doesn't have a name, but she may have buried it as well. These two names she just gave us today. She's starting to remember more and more. It's been three weeks or so since I found her. Dad said she would remember when she could, and he's right. I'm just afraid we're in for a torrent of information."

"I'm sure we will be." Redmond looked up from the material Rory had given them. "Dad, did you get a read on this?"

"I just had a chance to glance through it. Why?"

Redmond shared a look with his father before turning to Delaney. "Delaney, I am going to ask you to do something we don't normally." He slid the folder over in front of the younger man, younger by two years he had found out. "Will you look through this? You know the area. You know the people. We need your read on what is in this."

Delaney started to shake his head, until he looked towards the kitchen door, and sighed. He had to. For Regan's sake, if nothing more. They could not go on as a couple, if that's what she chose to do, until this was solved.

Chapter 16

Rising from his chair, his thoughts muddled, Delaney walked to the kitchen door, grabbing his jacket, Mick waiting for him. He had been two hours reading through the material, over and over, and he needed a break. He needed to think. He headed for his workshop, sorting through the tools of his trade, and placing them away. He wouldn't be needing them. Not for a while. He had no plans of going off to another dig. He had lost interest in that. Meeting Regan in a nearby town to his last dig had surprised him. The intensity of their emotions had overwhelmed them both, he thought. Lord, we sure seem to be in the middle of so many storms right now. Which one do we ride out? Which one do we run from? Which one will be the one that takes us down?

Mick stood up at him and whined, his tail wagging. Delaney looked down at him before he dropped to his knees and hugged Mick, his tears soaking into the dog's lush coat. Mick had been his constant companion for so many years now. His confidante, he thought. He knows my wants and wishes, my likes and dislikes, my dreams and disappointment. He knows how much I love Regan. He sat down finally, pulling Mick onto his knees, wrapping his arms tight around the dog, whose chin rested on his shoulder.

He prayed as he had never prayed before. He could feel the fury around him building and he knew he couldn't face it on his own. All the verses he could think of that spoke of comfort, of peace, of strength, of victory came to him.

He looked up as the door opened slowly and Tom walked in, studying him.

"Delaney? Your mom said you were out here."

Delaney sighed as he rose to his feet and stretched. "I just needed some space and time." He watched Tom closely, seeing something different about him that day. "Tom? You're not yourself."

Tom shook his head. "I'm not, Delaney. I came out today to ask you and Regan to forgive me."

"Forgive you? Why?"

Tom paced, gathering his thoughts. "You've known me all your life. My brother has always stayed away from your parents and you. I had no idea why. He's disappeared. I don't know where he is. When he hadn't called in two weeks, when he was supposed to, I went to his place and let myself in. Forgive me, Lord. I never knew." Tom paused to compose himself. "He was one of the ones who kidnapped your Regan. I didn't know that, Delaney, or I would have gone and found her. I called in a team to go through his place. I talked to a judge and obtained the proper search warrants. I have stepped back. Another detective has been brought in, this time from another force. We're turning the investigation over to them."

"Thank you, Tom." Delaney leaned against the workbench, watching as Tom settled down on a corner of the desk. "That means a lot to me. We will want to keep you close to us. I can't bring in someone else to help protect Regan. She's used to you. Someone new would set her back in her recovery."

Tom nodded. "I've cleared it that our force can still do that." He tilted his head. "You don't seem surprised at what I said."

Delaney shook his head. "To tell you the truth? Regan remembered two names today. One was your brother. The other is Baxter. Her family's been researching it. I'll let them know to turn over their results to the new detective." He blinked his eyes, feeling the grittiness of them. "She also remembered that she was bombarded with music and voices when she was on her own. She is afraid to sleep. Afraid the nightmares she suffered will return." He glanced towards the door. "Dad finally got me to agree to give her a sedative. She has refused, knowing she was drugged at times."

"I hate to ask. Has she said which one?"

"Which one what?"

"Which one attacked her that last day?"

Delaney sighed, knowing Tom was afraid it was his brother. "It was Baxter. And now we need to find him. I think he's been around here, trying to get in. Mick has been alerting to strange noises and I've seen evidence that someone is walking the perimeter of the property. And before you ask, Regan has refused to leave here. I can't make her."

Tom nodded. "That's what I wondered. Thank you for being honest, Delaney. I expected nothing less from you." He stood, his eyes on Mick. "Do you know where she was?"

"Rory came up with an address. It's outside of town."

"The old Berry place?"

"That's the one. I don't get the connection though with Baxter or Eric."

"There is one. Old Man Berry was Baxter's great-great-uncle. Not many people are aware of that. He refused to have anything to do with Baxter.

His house hasn't been lived in for years. The other force can go in and check it out."

"Riordan said he'd talk to them, but he wants to go out there first, to make sure it's the place she remembers."

"He's not taking Regan, is he?"

"No. I won't let him even if he wanted to. He'll take some photos." Delaney stood, shoved open the door and then locked it behind them. "It makes sense it would be that one. She said three floors, and it's near to Mom and Dad's. Too close. To think she was likely that close and I didn't know."

"Don't beat yourself up over something you can't change. God knew where she was and protected her." Tom held up a hand even as Delaney went to protest. "He did, and you know that. She could have died that day. I know, son, I know. She's been hurt in many ways. It's up to us to help her heal. With her memory coming back, she's heading that way herself."

Chapter 17

Regan paced the house, looking for Delaney. Mick paced beside her. It was late evening that day and she knew her father and brother had been there. She had peeked at the folder sitting on Delaney's desk. He had told her it was there. He had watched from the doorway and then walked away, knowing she would find him when she was ready to.

Delaney stood at the bottom of the staircase, watching her, seeing when she found him. His arms opened to wrap around her as she sought comfort from him, unable to stop the tremors running through her.

"I was that close, Delaney?" Her voice had hoarsened with her emotions.

"You were, my love. We didn't know that. We had no idea where you were. No one did. That's how hidden you were." He turned her towards the kitchen, pulling out a chair, and making her sit, reaching to make her tea and then setting a bowl of soup in front of her. "Eat, please, my love. Then, we'll talk."

Regan shoved her bowl away, contemplating eating more and then shaking her head. Her eyes found Delaney, who sat, head bowed in prayer, before she reached out a hand to touch him.

"Delaney?"

"Regan, how do we go on from here?" He watched her closely. "I don't want to lose you, and I'm afraid of just that happening if we don't find these men. Tom was by earlier. He's stepped out of the investigation but he'll continue to watch out for you."

"And for you." Regan rubbed at her face for a moment before she looked back at him. "Why did this happen? Do we know that? And was I taken for my sake or yours?"

"That's what your father and brothers are working on. They aren't sure. And I don't think I am either." He rose, heading for his office, and returning with two pads of paper and pens. "Here. You start listing whatever you can remember since we met at school. Names. Places. Events. Keep in mind what you have been doing as well. I'll do that from my perspective. When we're done, we'll look at each other's notes and see if we can find out anything."

She stared at the paper for a moment, her pen tapping against it. "That bomb threat. Who called it in? Do we know?"

Delaney reached for the folder sitting on the table, leafing through it. "It was anonymous, of course. When the authorities tried to track it, it went nowhere. They're still working on that but your Dad doesn't think they'll find out who it was." He looked up as she murmured. "Regan?"

"I think I know who." She looked up, tears sparkling in her eyes. "Do you remember that teacher that was in our Bible study group? The one no one liked. He was described as trying too hard."

"I do. Lewis Moran, wasn't it?"

"It was. Do you have your phone?"

Delaney was on his feet and heading for the conservatory, returning with both their phones. "Here's yours. Why?"

"I need to let Redmond or Dad know that name." Her fingers flew over the phone keyboard before she sat back. "I can see him doing something like this." She sipped at her tea, not noticing that it was now cold. Delaney shook his head as he took her mug and handed her a fresh cup.

She nodded her thanks, her attention on her notes, scribbling quickly whatever she remembered. She reached for a piece of the toast Delaney set in front of her.

He shook his head before he too became engrossed in his notes. He finally sat back, exhausted, raising his eyes to watch Regan. *Lord, she's remembering. Please? Don't let her be hurt. Help her to run to You for comfort and protection.*

"You're doing it again, Delaney."

"Doing what?"

"Praying with your eyes open. You're supposed to close your eyes when you pray."

"Says who?"

"Says our parents." She smirked at him. "Didn't they always say close your eyes and pray?"

He shook his head, his heart warming at the effort she was making to lighten their darkness. *That was the Regan he had fallen in love with. Please, Lord, let her return.*

She looked back down at her papers and then at her notes. "Delaney, I am seeing something here, but I'm not sure what. Dad sent me in with one of the boys. Over the years, I've done in about a dozen times. Each one was successful, except for that last one. And that one we couldn't get all the information we needed. Not in time."

Delaney looked up as she spoke. "Can you tell me the circumstances and the name?"

She searched his face, seeing his trust and belief in her on his face. "I can. Dad would if he was here. This is what happened. Rory and I were sent overseas to England. We had the name and address of a young woman who wanted to return home but was prevented from doing that. She had her passport and we were to go in, find her, and then fly home in a private jet. That's how we always do it. Dad has a pilot on retainer who works with us. He's clean. That much I can guarantee you.

"Anyway, we had trouble getting the information we needed to find her. Sometimes that happens, but this time, it seemed that we were being blocked. We finally were given the address she was at, but it was too late. She was dead. A drug overdose was the coroner's report. But she never used drugs, in fact, was adamant that she never would. She had no stigmata of a drug user. Dad thinks she was given an overdose the day before we found her. For some reason, she wasn't safe from whomever she was hiding from. They found her first. Dad is still working on that case, even though it's been months.

"Her name? You asked that. First, she was in her early 20's. She was from this area, I think Dad said."

Delaney's thoughts became chaotic when she said that. "Who was she, Regan?"

"Her name? Right. Her name. It was Val Easton."

"Val Easton?" Delaney shoved back from the table hard enough he had to reach for his chair. He almost ran for his office, returning with a book in his hand. He sat for a moment before he looked at Regan.

"Delaney? You're scaring me."

He could see the fear in her eyes and his heart broke. "I'm sorry. I shouldn't have done that." He looked down at the book in his hand. "This. This is the connection."

Regan reached for the book, her eyes on him. "You know he?"

He nodded. "I do. Her sister is married to a good friend of mine. I know her, not well, but yeah, she's from this town."

"We never had that information. I wonder if Tom said anything to Dad, but he not likely knew that's who it was. Dad doesn't give out that kind of information. The only reason I've told you is that we need to track what we were doing."

He nodded, even as he reached for her pad of paper, and handing her his. "Let's see what the other has written. He removed the pages he had written on, pulling back the pad of paper. "We need to note what we've found in common. I'm sure there will be lots."

At the end of two hours, Regan sat back, exhausted to the point she didn't know if she could even rise from the chair. Delaney's head was bent over the papers before he looked up. He laid down his pen and rose, reaching to pull back her chair and scooping her into his arms. Her head on his shoulder, her eyes closed as she drifted off to sleep, for once feeling safe and secure. He hesitated and looked at the stairs and then headed for the conservatory, gently laying her on the mattress and pulling the blankets up over her. He stretched out as well, Mick at their feet, and decided he would lay there for five minutes and then get up and shut off lights.

Chapter 18

Her eyes cracking open slowly early the next morning, Regan lay still for a moment, her thoughts drifting over the past couple of months. She realized she didn't have the deep fear or terror that she had been experiencing. What Delaney had had her do the night before, going back over everything like they had, had helped. She reached for Mick, finding him tight to her. She smiled. Delaney complained that he had lost his dog, but always with a smile on his face, and usually a quick hug. Mick had been a blessing to her, helping to calm her and to heal her. She rubbed at his ears for a moment before she turned, feeling a weight across her.

Delaney still slept, his arm across Regan. She studied him for a moment, knowing her love for him was still there, but afraid that he would suffer because of her. She knew that both Rory and Leah and Reilly and Aideen had suffered because of the other, almost losing Reilly during Rory's adventure as it was now termed. She shuddered, thinking adventure was a misnomer, that it had been much worse. She shoved at Mick and then rose, her eyes on Delaney before she headed for the stairs and her bedroom. She needed clean clothes, but first a shower, she thought, her hand trailing up the dark oak handrail. She paused for a moment, studying the entryway and what she could see of the rooms from where she stood part-way up the stairs. She had come to love this home and prayed that she would not have to leave it.

She turned from the door of the kitchen, shutting it after Mick, before she headed for the counter. It was time she took back her life, she thought. Those men had taken too much from her. She felt her throat, knowing that it was still healing. She prayed, asking God for a touch from the garment, for healing, but if no healing, for peace and acceptance of where she was physically.

She set her mug down on the table, reaching to tidy up the papers they had left laying there the night before. She looked up and then rose, finding the light switch to turn off the lights. Delaney must have been asleep right after me, she thought. It's not like him to leave so many lights on. She knew what they were going through was wearing on him as well. She wanted this over and over now, before he headed to the classroom and his new duty of professor.

She reached for the papers once more, her hands still as she sorted through them, finally taking time to read through each one. Her hand reached for paper and pen, and she started jotting down ideas and thoughts.

She sat back, a frown on her face. No, she thought. It wasn't to do with that last trip, even though it was connected to here. Someone was after her father and she just didn't know who. That was what had been bothering her about Rory and Reilly. There was something unexplained about what they went through, had always been, despite the police finishing off their investigation and closing the cases.

She looked up as she felt a hand on her shoulder. Delaney stood watching her before he dropped kiss on the top of her head. She leaned into him for a moment, her eyes searching him.

"I'll get breakfast, now that you're up. Go on. Get cleaned up." She shoved at him, making him move back. As she stood, he wrapped her into a tight hug.

"I'll do that. I see you made it up the stairs." He stood for a moment, his eyes trained on the top of her head. "Welcome back, sweetheart. Last night seems to have helped."

"It did." She leaned back to look up at him. "Now, go. I can't get breakfast if you don't let me go." She watched as mischief sparkled on his face. "Delaney?"

"I'm going." He watched her for a moment. "Regan, no matter what happens, or where we go, just know that I love you deeply." With that, he walked away, leaving her staring after him, hope sparking in her heart that just maybe they could salvage their relationship.

An hour later, the kitchen cleaned from their meal, Regan turned, her eyes on the piles of paper they had set to one side before she slid back into her chair.

"What day is it anyway?"

Delaney looked up, his mind needing time to absorb her words. "It's Sunday." He groaned and reached for his phone. "The worship team I'm on has their turn this Sunday." He scrolled through his contacts, looking for the leader's number, when Regan's hand closed over his. He looked up at her.

"We're not hiding. Not anymore." He had to listen to catch her words, knowing that she was trying to express herself in a way that didn't offend him.

"Are you sure? We don't have to go."

She shot a look at the clock. "We don't have to. We need to. At least, I do. I need to sit and absorb the music, the scripture for the day, the very atmosphere of being in God's house. Do you understand what I'm trying to say and not succeeding very well?"

Delaney reached to hug her. "I do. I need that too. We have to leave in about thirty minutes, if you're ready."

"That I am, Delaney." She frowned. "I have to replace my purse. For some reason, I have my identification, but not the purse I had that day. And my carryon bag is missing."

"Tom asked about what you had that day. He brought your luggage here for you. But you haven't opened it yet."

"I will. I guess I have no choice." She started to rise, but Delaney's hand on her arm kept her still.

"Later, Regan. This afternoon, we'll go through it."

She nodded before she rose, heading to let Mick out. "We can do that. Somehow, I think something is in that bag, and I'm afraid to open it."

Two hours later, Regan stood tight to Delaney, his arm around her as he greeted his friends, introducing her to them, garnering them both looks of disbelief, shock, and acceptance. Her memory clicked in and she drew in a deep breath. There had been one of his friends there that day they had married. He hadn't seen the woman, but she had. She would never forget the look of pure venom that was directed at her.

Delaney felt her stiffen and knew he had to get her out of there. He excused them and turned her to the front of the sanctuary, leading her through a door and then down a hallway before he opened a door to the outside, near his car. He tucked her inside, stopping for a moment, an unsettled feeling running through him, shivers at the feeling of being watched shaking him slightly.

Late that afternoon, Regan went looking for Delaney, not finding him anywhere in the house. She closed and locked the door behind her, heading for his workshop. He might be there, she thought. She stood for a moment, her hand on the door knob, before she pulled the door open and entered, finding Delaney sorting through papers on his desk.

Delaney looked up as he heard the door, his hands stopping their movement, before he rose and walked towards Regan, his head tilted as he searched her face.

"Regan?"

She wrapped her arms around him, feeling his around her. "I think there is someone else, Delaney. Someone over these two. I can remember hearing another voice. A woman's. Does that make sense?"

He looked down at her. "It does, in a bizarre way. I didn't think these were the only two. There had to be someone behind them. Neither man had the financial means to do what they did."

"And it would take money, wouldn't it? They had to be paid, else they wouldn't have taken me and kept me."

"No, they wouldn't have. Is that why you came looking for me?"

She nodded. "I found something disturbing in what we were doing. It goes deeper than just someone after you and I."

He turned her towards the door, despite her protest that he needed to work there.

"No, I was almost done. Another couple of hours on another day will finish that. I want to see what you found."

Chapter 19

Delaney stood, staring down at the sheet of paper Regan handed him, not quite sure of where she had been heading when she discovered this.

"How did you do this again?" He looked up, knowing she was frustrated.

"I told you. I was putting names together with dates and places, and that one kept coming up."

"I didn't realize you knew her as well."

"Well, I do." She sounded disgruntled and sighed, knowing she had just taken her frustration out on Delaney. She opened her mouth to apologize and then snapped it shut as he shook his head. "I think she was there all the time on the edges of any group or event we were at. I don't remember her, but something tells me she was."

"You are correct in that. I remember seeing her at some of the events, but I didn't think anything about it. After all, they were events anyone could attend." He made her sit, sitting beside her, reaching for her hands, knowing they needed to make this a matter of prayer. If they were correct, and he had no doubt that they were, things had just gotten worse and stranger.

"How is she related to the town?"

"I'm not sure she is. Let's pass this on to Rory. He can work on it for you. First, though, we need to pray and pray hard. Tom has said the investigators can't find either Baxter or Eric. They're hiding. I fear that they will come after you again."

Heads bent, Delaney prayed, begging for protection for his bride, and a fast resolution to what was going on, keeping in mind he had to pray for God's will in this, no matter how hard that was. He looked up when he finished, studying Regan's face before her eyes opened. She had a look in them he couldn't read.

"Don't, Regan."

"Don't what?"

"Don't put yourself out there. At least, not without me."

"I know, Delaney. I know I can't but who knows how long this will go on unless we come up with a plan and implement it."

"That's what I'm afraid of. Your plans." He grinned as she playfully swatted at him. He reached for the papers she had been writing on that day and read through them. "You've come up with a lot of information here."

"I know. I took pictures and sent them on to Rory. Hopefully he can make some kind of sense from them. I didn't go to Dad. He's too close in some ways."

"He is. Rory may be as well but he doesn't know Tom or Eric, so that helps. Your Dad said he hadn't brought his family over since Ryanne was a few months old."

"No, he never did. He would never say why, though."

"Would he tell you now?"

She shrugged. "I doubt it. Whatever happened had to have been bad enough that Dad didn't want us here." She turned to look at him. "Would your parents know?"

"We can ask. Mom wants us to come for dinner tomorrow night."

"That works." Regan slumped back in her chair, her eyes on her folded hands. "Delaney, where do we go from here? I mean us, as a couple."

The ringing of the doorbell precluded his answering her question, and that frustrated him. He pulled the door open quicker than he meant to, finding Rory standing there."

"Rory? What are you doing here?"

A grim look on his face, Rory pointed into the house. "Can we go in, please? I need to talk to you both."

Regan stood in the kitchen, staring at her brother. "I just sent you that material two hours ago. You haven't had time to look through it. It takes you an hour to get here."

"I know. I scrolled through what you sent. How did you ever connect all this?"

"I don't know. It just all seemed to fit together this afternoon."

"And do you realize the danger you are under, just from having done that?" Rory bit his words out, worry for his sister uppermost in his mind.

"Don't snipe at me, Rory. I know we're still under danger and will be until these people are caught."

"You don't get it, Regan. It's not just this. Whoever took you was trying to get to Delaney too. He found something somewhere on one of his trips that they want. That's the scuttlebutt I'm hearing."

She moved back from him, right into Delaney who wrapped his arms around her.

“Rory? Can we sit? You have information, I’m guessing. Talk to us. Don’t scare your sister.”

Rory stared at him, catching the warning in Delaney’s eyes. “Yes, we need to sit. Neither one of you will like what I have to say. I ran it by Dad on my way over here. He’s concerned enough he wants to find a security team for you two.”

Regan glared at him. “You can tell Dad that’s not happening. I refuse to hide anymore. Delaney and I are going to go on living our lives. What happens happens.”

Rory shook his head even as he reached for the folder he had dropped on the table, his eyes taking in the piles of paper already on the tabletop. “You two have been busy.”

“We have been. Doing this helped, Rory. I slept last night without any dreams.” Regan’s voice was barely above a whisper at that point.

“You did? I’m glad.” Rory paused to pray, before he opened the folder. “That name, Regan? How close was she to you two?”

Delaney spoke up. “Not very. We can remember seeing her around but we never had contact with her. At least, not that we remember.”

“That’s what I thought. For some reason, she has fixated on you, Delaney. That reason we’re still trying to work through and not getting anywhere too quickly. Word I have received is that she is dangerous to those she had taken a dislike too. Regan, you’re on her radar. It has to be because of Delaney.”

“No, I don’t think so. I mean, not really.” Regan turned to watch Delaney, her eyes searching his face. “I think it was something he found on one of his digs He’s only been on what, three, Delaney?”

"That's correct. And any artifacts I found I have turned over to the proper authorities. I kept nothing."

"Is that a known fact?"

"It should be. I have done interviews and emphasized that I kept nothing." His voice died away as his eyes closed. "It was this last dig, Rory. I found something buried there that didn't belong. A small decorative chest. I turned it over to the police. They told me it was stolen and I had to do some fast talking to convince them it wasn't me. Is that what she's after?"

Rory shrugged. "It could be. Did you look in the chest at all? And just how big was it?"

"It was small, maybe six inches all over. And no, I didn't open it. I knew it was too modern for what we were finding. I left the site right away and headed for the police. I wasn't sure if there had been thefts going on or not. That being buried there? It had to have been within the last ten years, going by the style of the chest."

Rory nodded again. "We didn't think you did. I called the police department you stopped at. They were shocked to hear of what had happened and are willing to work with us. The detective I spoke to sent me what he could of the investigation. Again, Delaney? You did not open the box? You have no idea what was in it?"

Delaney shook his head, feeling Regan's hand reach for his and tighten on it. He looked at her, missing the speculative look on Rory's face. "No, once again, I didn't. I just knew I didn't want to know what was in it."

Rory sighed. "That's what I was told. The detective was quite open about his talks over the few days with you. I gather they never told you what was in it?"

Delaney stared at Rory. "No, they never did. Should they have?"

Sighing, Rory opened the folder and silently handed Delaney a picture. He heard the sharp intake of breath from Regan and knew that things had just intensified and gotten worse for his sister. How did they keep the couple safe?

Chapter 20

Delaney stared at the photo he had been handed, feeling Regan's hand on his, turning it so she could see too. He heard her sharp intake of breath.

"Is this for real? It can't be that old then. That's Regan and I on the dig site. About two weeks after we connected, wasn't it?"

"It was. I don't remember seeing anyone around that stood out but there were a number of people there working. I can remember the security people working to keep bystanders well away." She looked at her brother. "Is it one of the workers who did this?"

"That's what we're looking into. We have obtained all the names. Together with the detective from there, we'll be working through this. Given what has happened here, he asked if we could have someone else work on this as well. Paul volunteered."

"He's good at that." Regan paused. "Rory, do you remember that couple we met a few years ago? When we were overseas?"

"Emma and Abe? I do. Why? You won't take a security team and that's what he does?"

"Not Abe. Emma. Did she ever tell you what she does?"

Rory shook his head. "Not that I recall. Why?"

"You have heard of Trackers, I know that. You've mentioned them. Emma is Tracker. Send the names on to her, or I will. She and her team can find out so much more than we can. I have no idea how she does it. Abe told me that her mind is scary and that not many people can follow her train of thought.”

Rory stared at his sister. "I never knew that. She is so humble and quiet about what she does. I thought she worked for Abe or for her brother who’s the investigator.”

Regan looked at Delaney, realizing she had shut him out. She went on to explain about Trackers and Abe and Emma.

“They can find information for us?”

“I’m sure that they can.” Rory narrowed his eyes. “You’ve already been in touch, haven’t you, Regan?”

“I did. We’ve kept in contact over the years. I treasure her friendship. She’s been helping walk me through what I went through. She has told me of their “adventure” as she calls it. Did you know his whole team went through stuff as did a number of their friends?”

Rory threw up his hands. “No. How would I? No one talked to me about that.”

“Rory, stuff a sock in it.”

Delaney drew in a deep breath and then began to laugh, knowing Regan was becoming more like herself. “I think you just got told, Rory. Regan, has this Emma been in touch?”

“Just to say she had the information and once she knew more, she’d call.” Regan looked up as the doorbell rang. “What is going on today?”

Delaney stood at the open door, taking in the blond-haired man and the lady with the russet hair before he spoke.

"Can I help you?"

"If you are Delaney Callahan and married to Regan, then you can." The man reached to shake Delaney's hand. "I'm Abe Finlay and this is my wife, Emma."

Delaney stared at them, shock on his face. "How'd you do that?"

The couple shared a look before Abe spoke, watching Delaney as he leaned back against the closed door. "Do what?"

"Emma? Abe?" Regan's voice had them turning, Emma across the hardwood floor of the entryway to draw Regan into a tight hug, Abe following her. "What are you two doing here? I just sent you that stuff early this morning."

"Emma and Jace worked all morning. Jace is still working through research. Ian flew us in." He turned to Delaney. "Is that the airport that had the bomb threat?"

"It is. That's what we can't figure out. It's too small an airport to have a lot of traffic through it. We had to change flights in a larger city."

"Come on into the kitchen. Rory's here and has information as well."

Abe and Emma settled down, watching the other three closely, Emma knowing that her research would send them off on another tangent.

"Bring us up to date on what you have, please, Rory." Emma's voice was quiet but composed.

Rory stared at her for a moment before he handed over his folder. "Here. This is what I've come up with. Paul, at our office, was still working on stuff."

Abe began to laugh. "Stuff? Very descriptive there. Covers a whole lot."

Emma swatted his arm. "Abe. Behave yourself. Next time, I'll leave you at home with Isaac and you can babysit your own son."

Abe continued to grin. "That I would enjoy." He looked over at Delaney, who was watching the couple with interest. "Isaac's our son. Looks like his momma."

"And has his father's temperament." Emma commented even as she read rapidly through the material before she sat back, her eyes on the wall behind Rory before she looked at him. "You're good, Rory. I'd hire you in a flash if you ever want more work. You think outside the box."

Regan laughed hard at that. "He always has. That always got him into a lot of trouble."

"Now the truth is out. And you didn't, I suppose, Mrs. Callahan?" Delaney was delighted to hear Regan's laugh freely and joke with her brother. She was progressing in her healing, he thought.

"No. Never. I was the perfect angel child, I'll have you know." She looked over at Rory with a grin as he snorted. "Stop, Rory. You know what Mom would say about that."

"And I know what she would say about your comment. Perfect angel child. Who thought up so much of what we got into?"

"Reilly."

"Very convenient. He's not here to defend himself."

Emma looked at the two of them, shaking her head, hiding her own laughter, knowing that Rory was deliberately baiting his sister and she was responding in kind. From what she understood, it was time for that to happen. She watched as Delaney's eyes bounced back and forth between the siblings and a small frown lined her face.

Abe spoke from beside her, soft enough that only she could hear. "Delaney never met her family until now from what I understand."

"He didn't? So this is all new to him." She pondered that for a moment before her attention went back to her papers and she spoke. "Okay, people. Let's figure out what we can. We need to get moving on this because I am hearing of threats against both of you."

"Threats? What kind of threats?" Delaney finally spoke, his eyes on Emma.

"Death threats for one." Emma looked with compassion as his eyes slid closed. "On both of you. Do you have any idea why?"

Delaney shook his head. "Not off hand. I would say that the chest I found a few weeks ago plays into it."

"What chest?" Emma flipped through her paperwork. "I don't see anything about a chest you found. Wasn't I told?"

"We just were talking about that. Rory actually tracked down the detective who is still working on it." Delaney drew in a deep breath. "Here. This is a photo of what was in it. When I found it, I just turned it over to the police. I never opened it, so I had no idea what was in it. All I knew what that it was wrong for the time frame of the dig."

Emma reached for it, reading it and then handing it back. "That's what I've been told. This threat was before Regan disappeared? That's correct?"

"It is." Regan's voice had dropped in volume and she had to swallow hard to continue. "It was even before we were married." Her eyes on Delaney, she continued. "Who does this? Who threatens to kill someone but doesn't say why?"

"We've seen it far too often, Regan." Abe spoke up. "In my line of work, it can be a common tool. You are directly named in that, Regan. Plans were being made even at that point to remove from Delaney's life. Did anyone know you were planning on getting married?"

Delaney shook his head. "No. We didn't decide until about a week after I found that. Where we were, we could get our license and then marry that day. That's what we did."

Regan nodded, watching Abe closely, wondering where his comments was taking the search. "Abe? You have thoughts?"

"I do, Regan. Rory, you said you had a name?" He took the paper, reading it before handing it silently to Emma, who nodded.

"She's the one. What we're having difficulty doing is finding out anything about her. There is no history of her before she was 19. That was when she appeared in your life, you two."

"No history? How can that be?"

"That is an interesting question. Jace is running a search for me based on her picture and what we know about her." She paused as her phone vibrated. "And that is Jace now." She excused herself and walked away, leaving the four staring after her.

"Does she always do that?" Rory just shook his head.

"She can.   She's intense when she's researching something involving friends. I have to make her stop and eat and sleep. Having Isaac has helped. He comes first over any investigation."

"But you're here."   Regan's protest echoed through the room as Emma returned, sliding into her seat, notes she had scrawled quickly in front of her. "Emma?"

"I have news that I am not sure how to share with you."

Chapter 21

Regan stared at Emma, not sure if she was serious. "Emma, what did you find?"

Emma shared a look with Abe, who nodded. Abe didn't need to know the information to know that Emma was very concerned about how it would be taken.

"Regan. Delaney. The lady who seems to be tracking you? She is connected to this town. She is cousin to Val Easton."

"Val Easton? Oh no! Now, I see the connection!" Regan shoved her chair back and ran from the room. Delaney could hear her steps on the stairs and then along the hallway above them, Mick's nails clicking in time with her.

"Delaney? Care to explain?"

Rory spoke up. "Val Easton! Now how does she come into this? Sorry, Abe. Emma. We knew of her but she was dead before we could speak with her. That took a lot from Regan."

"And from you, Rory." Delaney paused. "I know Val as her sister is married to a friend of mine. I didn't know her that well though."

"So who is this lady?" Regan watched Emma closely. "You say she's a cousin of this Val Easton."

"That is what we're hearing but Jace isn't comfortable with that. He's still searching." Emma sighed as her phone vibrated again. "Jace, what did you find?" Emma started to write rapidly as she listened with few words on her part. She thoughtfully set her phone now before she looked at the younger couple, her eyes taking in Rory as well.

"Emma? What did he say?" Delaney watched her closely.

"He is still looking. He did find out that she wasn't a cousin after all. That was a cover she set up."

"A cover? Just who is she?"

"That's what we can't find out. It's like she didn't exist before age 19. Don't worry. We'll find her." She looked down at her notes. "We have to leave soon. We have commitments we need to get to. We wanted to meet with you, find out what you're facing and then offer our help. Rory. This folder has what we have so far. Jace knows to call you with whatever he is finding, as well as relaying it to me. Delaney. Regan. You two need to take precautions. You are far from safe."

Abe grinned. "Ian, my pilot and one of my men, has offered to fly you two wherever you'd like to go, until we can find the people responsible."

"That won't work. It never does. They would stay in hiding until we returned." Regan stood as the older couple did and walked with them to the door. Rory and Delaney watched and then turned to the paperwork laying on the table in front of them.

"Rory? What are we missing? There has to be something we have."

Rory looked up briefly, considered Delaney's words, shook his head and immersed himself once more into the research. Delaney sighed and then rose, heading for his office. Sunday and all, he needed to start working on lesson plans. He had thought to have had the semester laid out already and he was from that goal.

Regan watched for a moment as Delaney sat, unaware she was in the doorway. Rory, she knew, would not answer if she were to interrupt him. He was like that when he was working. She sighed, looking down at Mick.

"It's just you and me, Mick. What shall we do? Come on. You've been inside all day. You need some fresh air and so do I."

Regan stood for a moment on the back porch and then walked down the steps and out into the yard. The snow had melted enough that she could see the gardens around the yard and the fountain in the middle of it. She walked to the fountain, reaching to touch the concrete and then stepping back.

She heard Mick's sudden growl before he yelped. As she spun, she felt arms around her and a hand over her mouth. She fought to get away, unsuccessful as she has carried around the house and stuffed into a vehicle, a blindfold over her eyes and a gag in her mouth before her hands were bound in front of her. She still fought hard until she felt the slightest prick on her arm and the sounds around her faded into darkness.

Delaney looked up from his work and then was on his feet, running for the outdoors, Rory standing as he ran by and then following him. Delaney dropped to his knees beside Mick and then looked around.

"Where's Regan?"

Rory spun and then carefully followed the footsteps in what little snow remained and in the soft dirt. "She's disappeared." Rory slid to a stop, his eyes on the vehicle leaving, memorizing the plate number.

Delaney stopped beside him. "Mick's okay, I think. He's on his feet. Where is she?"

Rory nodded into the distance. "In that vehicle that just disappeared." His phone was out as he called for help, his hand on Delaney's arm as he steered him back to the front porch.

"Rory?"

Rory kept his hand up as he gave the information he had, finally slipping his phone into his pocket. "Inside, Delaney. They want you inside."

"No. I want to go after Regan." He moved towards the stairs, Rory's hand on his chest stopping him.

"We have to. They don't want the scene contaminated. Now, where's Mick?"

"Likely at the back door." Delaney almost ran through the house, pulling the door open and scooping Mick into his arms, slamming the door closed before he sank down, his hands searching for any wounds on his dog.

Mick whined, wriggled to get free, and then attacked the kitchen door, wanting back out to find his Regan. He knew she was in danger and he wanted to help her.

Tom stood, finally free to find Delaney, watching as his young friend paced. His heart hurt for him and he prayed fervently that they would find Regan and find her soon. He didn't know how long Delaney would be able to keep moving, his energy level was at such a high peak. He would crash soon, that Tom knew.

He looked at Rory who shook his head and pointed towards the conservatory. Tom followed him, not sure what was up.

"Regan had friends here today. They left a lot of material for you."

"But I'm not the investigating officer, not ." Tom protested, even though he was curious as to what was left.

"They know that. They've cleared it for you to have a copy." Rory glanced towards the doorway. "Regan and Delaney did a lot of work yesterday as well. I have a copy of it all for you."

"Can you briefly tell me?"

"I can. Whoever it is that took Regan in the first place is a female. She was watching them. We don't know why yet or who she actually is. She was using an alias that was totally fabricated."

"I see. That's why we've been stonewalled then."

"It is. And it all seems to relate back to that bad situation Regan and I were on. Only I'm not sure how. You would think they would be after Dad for that."

Tom paused, then reached to take the material. "That you would think. How is Delaney right now?"

Rory shrugged. "I don't know him well enough to gauge, but I know when Leah went missing, I was devastated. I couldn't eat, couldn't sleep, paced, tried to think of where she was."

Tom nodded. "Let me look through this. Maybe, knowing the town and its people, I'll see something."

"That's what we're hoping, Tom. Thank you."

Chapter 22

Her eyes opening slowly, Regan roused, listening for any life around her. She heard nothing and then sat up abruptly, her eyes closing as her head spun. She finally made it to her feet, her hand going out to brace herself against the wall. She blinked to clear her eyes, feeling the dryness of her throat. Not again, she thought. Please, Lord? Wasn't once enough? Why twice?

She felt her away around the room, the darkness broken by the light of the moon as it shone through the windows. She paused at the door, hesitant to try it, and then reached for the knob, finding it turning under her hand.

She frowned. There is no way they'd do this twice, was there? She pulled the door open slowly and peeked out. She was on a main floor, she could tell. That she was glad of. She stepped back into the room, closing the door softly, feeling that if she went out that way, she would be in danger.

She turned, her eyes on the windows and moved towards them. She felt for the lock, and then shoved at the window, surprised that it moved upwards. She stuck her head out, peering through the darkness before she was over the sill, dropping to the ground, and then jumping up to catch the bottom of the window and pull it down to hide her escape.

She crept towards the building behind where she was, her hand reaching out to touch the rough cement blocks before she felt her way around it, to find herself near the downtown area of Whitlock. This is strange, she thought. I would have suspected I would be taken out of town again.

She made her way on silent feet, her arms around herself to keep herself warm. She knew where she was, but didn't have any means of phoning Delaney. She paused in the shadows as she saw a vehicle approaching and then she was at the curb, flagging down the patrol car.

The female officer was out of her vehicle, around to Regan, assessing her, asking her quick questions before she opened the door and waited for Regan to sit before she was around and behind the wheel, heading for Delaney's house. She reached for the radio when Regan shook her head.

"Please? Can we just go there?"

The officer gave her a quick glance and then nodded. By the time she called it in, she knew she would have Regan home.

Regan stared at the commotion and vehicles surrounding her home and turned to the officer.

"What is going on?"

The officer looked at her and then smiled. "This is all for you, Regan. We're trying to find you. Instead you found me. Now you're home. Here, let's get you inside."

The officer shoved at the door, letting Regan step into the house, her eyes searching for Delaney, not seeing him at first, but instead finding Mick running towards her, jumping up as she stooped over to hug him, taking the frantic kisses he was giving. The officers in the house turned and she heard someone calling for Tom.

She ignored them all, almost running as she went through the house, stopping just inside the doorway of Delaney's office, seeing him at his desk, his head on his arms. She didn't hear Rory's softly breathed "Regan" behind her as she moved forward, a hand going out to touch Delaney on the head.

Delaney froze. He knew that touch, but it wasn't possible. She was missing. He would have heard if she had been found. He raised up, blinking in confusion for a moment as he stared at the woman standing there before he was on his feet, Regan wrapped in his arms, sobs shaking both their bodies.

He finally stood her back, hands cupping her shoulders as he searched her face. "How?"

She shrugged. "They left the door unlocked, but I was too scared to go that way. God wouldn't let me. I slipped out a window, walked a bit and found an officer who brought me home. I wasn't that far away, Delaney. Downtown, near the library I think."

She hadn't heard Tom behind her or see him jerk with surprise and then spin, walking rapidly away, already barking orders and she didn't see the officers running to search the house. Tom sent the officer who had brought Regan home to find the judge, knowing he had search warrants ready for them, just needing the address.

Rory stood, watching his sister before Delaney spoke quietly to her and she turned, her eyes on her brother before he touch had her in a tight grip.

"I was so scared, Regan. I didn't want to have to tell Dad you were missing again."

"How long?"

Rory frowned, his eyes on Delaney. "How long? What do you mean?"

"How long was I gone this time? I know I was drugged but how long?"

Rory shrugged. "Four hours, five at the most."

She broke away from him, pacing the room, finally standing in front of Delaney. "This makes no sense, Delaney. Why take me and then let me walk away? That just doesn't happen."

"Can you tell us anything at all, Regan?" Tom's voice brought her attention to him.

She shook her head. "Not really. It was dark so I didn't get a good look at the room or the building. I just knew that I couldn't go out the door. Danger was waiting out there."

Tom turned as his phone rang, and he excused himself to walk away, spinning to stare at Regan. He pocketed his phone and stood, his eyes on her.

"Tom? What happened? You're scaring me." Regan moved to stand near him, Delaney's arm around her as he stood beside her, Rory on her other side.

"You have no idea why you couldn't go out that door? None at all?"

She shook her head. "None. It was like God had put up a gate and wouldn't unlock it for me. I just knew I couldn't go that way. Why?"

Tom shook his head. "I had to pull the officers out. There was a bomb set to go off if you had stepped just outside that door. Again, Regan? How did you know?"

She stared at him, before she waved her hands in the air. "I told you. I will not repeat myself. Whether you believe me or not, that's what happened. And no, I am not part of some deep dark conspiracy to get at Delaney or even my Dad." She broke away from Delaney and almost ran from the room.

Delaney listed to her footsteps as she ran up the stairs and turned to Tom. "She's told you the truth, Tom. I won't have you questioning her statement. Accept it for what it is. When you can, check the windows. You'll find evidence just as she said."

Tom rubbed at the back of his neck. "I know, Delaney. I know. It's just too bizarre. She was that close to not coming home." He stared between the two younger men. "I know she won't remember who or what, but if she can't, then you know as well as I that people will say she's part of it."

"She isn't. We'll do everything we can to get that word around, including an interview with the paper." Delaney paused, sensing movement from Rory. "Maybe that's what we should do."

"Wait, Delaney. You don't want to do that."

"I'm sorry, Tom. We will do what we need to so that we can end this. We can't go on with our lives, make plans, see where God wants us with this over us." Delaney walked away, his tread measured and slow, as he headed to find Regan.

Rory watched him go before looking at Tom. "Tom? What didn't you say?"

"What do you mean?"

"There was more. Why would you question Regan like that if there wasn't."

Tom sighed. "There was. There was a letter, purported to be from Regan to Delaney, admitting her involvement in all this. But that isn't her."

"Was it handwritten?" When Tom nodded, Rory sighed. "Compare her handwriting to it. It won't match."

"Don't you think I know that? But people will talk, no matter what we do."

"I know. That's why I think Delaney has the right idea."

"If they do that, they should work with our PR people. They can help." Tom walked away, leaving Rory staring after him before he nodded, his hand reaching to ruffle Mick's ears at the dog stood up at him, unsettled because of the commotion in his home.

Chapter 23

Delaney stood for a moment in the doorway of the room Regan had chosen, knowing she had like the soft jades and creams he had chosen for it. The antique furniture suited the colouring. He moved towards where she stood in the middle of the room, stopping short.

"Regan?"

"What?" She sighed, knowing she had bitten her words out. "I'm sorry, sweetheart. It's not your fault. Nor is it mine." She looked fierce for a moment. "I think I have been blaming myself and I shouldn't. I didn't do anything, other than declare my love for you and agree to marry you."

"And that seems to be the problem." He reached to pull her close and then stopped. "They will want the clothes you have on, including the shoes." He looked down at the low heels she seemed to favour. "How did you ever manage with those shoes?"

She looked down even as she shrugged. "I didn't walk that far and when I dropped out of the window, it was into snow." She looked up. "There's something odd about all this. Tom knows more than what he's told us."

"He does." Delaney turned her towards the ensuite bathroom. "Go on. Have a shower or a bath. I'll stand guard."

She stared over her shoulder at him for a moment, catching a glance on his face that gave her pause but yet hope. She knew he loved her deeply as she did him. She paused, her hand on her head, as she thought through what she needed.

"Go on, love. I'll find some clothes for you and leave them on the vanity. And then I will set myself down here in that chair by the door and not let you be disturbed." He reached under the vanity for a garbage bag. "Here. Use this for your skirt and sweater and shoes. I'll give it to Tom. But I highly doubt this will help. Not after us hugging you."

Regan stood after she had showered and dressed, looking down at the clothes Delaney had found for her. Somehow he had known just what to find. A favourite cord skirt in brown and a deep rust sweater. She knew people would say she should not wear rust with red hair, but she didn't care. She needed the comfort these clothes brought her and the comfort knowing that Delaney had taken the time to find her favourites. She peered at her feet. No shoes but slippers. That was okay. Her feet were sore from what she had been through.

She watched from the doorway as Delaney sat, his head back on the chair, his eyes closed. He wasn't sleeping, she knew somehow. He was praying. She could feel those prayers. He looked up as she moved towards him, standing and wrapping her into his arms. He is so tall, she thought, taller than my brothers and father. I always vowed that I would never marry someone so tall. But that's part of who he is. Height doesn't matter. It's his character, his love of God, his love for her, and his trust in her that kept her striving to solve what was happening to them. Her throat was sore and she knew that she soon had to deal with that, but right now, she was where she needed to be and where she wanted to be.

Chapter 24

Two days later, Delaney ran through the house, searching for Regan. He had heard her scream and feared the worst. He found her standing on the front porch, shaking, Mick in front of her pushing her back towards the door.

"Regan?"

She spun and launched herself at him. "They were here, Delaney. They've been here. There is writing on the garage door. Why won't they leave us alone?" Sobs shook her body as he scooped her into his arms and carried her back inside, Mick running with them, and used his foot to slam the door closed. He sank down on the stairs, keeping her wrapped in his arms.

"How bad was it?"

She shuddered. "It was a date, Delaney. A date that said was the day I would die." She sobbed, her voice gone before she could finish.

She finally calmed down enough that Delaney could reach for his phone and make another call to the police about another situation. He sighed. They would soon be tired of hearing from them. Then, he paused. How did he know that someone on the town's force wasn't working for whoever it was? It was all so vague, but someone had to be watching them closely. He didn't have near neighbours, at least none that he would say was doing just that.

Tom stood, once more, facing Delaney's home, a frown on his face as he read the words spray painted in red on the door. He shook his head as he listened to the tech working the scene.

"Did you get all the pictures you could?"

"I did. This is not what they needed. Not with what she's gone through."

"No, it isn't. Look, I know we're not investigating but I have been given permission to be kept updated as it does affect their safety. Let me know what you find out." Tom walked away, heading for the steps, finding Delaney waiting for him.

"How's Regan?"

"How would you expect her to be?" Delaney's anger flared. "Find whoever it is, Tom. This is destroying her and in destroying her, destroying me and our marriage. I want this over. Yesterday."

"We all do, Delaney. Not just for your sakes. This is stressing out the force and they want it over for you too."

Delaney nodded, before spinning on his heel and stalking back into the house, leaving Tom staring at him. This was not the Delaney he knew, and he could completely understand what he was going through. He had seen it before but not this bad.

Tom found Regan in the kitchen, her back to the door as she worked away. He tilted his head to watch, shaking it as he saw that she was not really doing anything, other than making a mess.

"Don't say a word, Tom. I know I'm making a mess. It's exactly what I wanted to do." She stopped, blinking rapidly. "How do you find who's responsible? I want this stopped and stopped now."

Tom nodded as he leaned a hip against the counter, facing her, seeing how she was struggling. His heart broke for her and he knew he needed to get either her mother or father there.

“Who do you want to come?”

“What do you mean? I don’t want anyone to come.” She felt Delaney’s arms come around her and just hold her. “If anyone came, they would be in danger. I can’t ask that of them.”

“It doesn’t matter to them, love. They want to be part of this. They were with Rory and Reilly. Do you think they would want less for you? You need their support. I need their support. We have my parents here. Tom’s here. But it’s not your family. So, as Tom asked, who do you want?”

“I just need my Mom.” The men could hardly hear her. They heard the fear in her voice, but the deep desperate need for a young girl for her mother. Tom knew it didn’t matter how old a woman was. She would always need her mother, in many cases. He knew Naomi and Regan were close and that in a case like this, he would make the call.

He pulled out his phone, his eyes on Regan as she watched him. “Tell me no, Regan, and I won’t call. But I know your Mom. She would want to be here. You have that self-contained apartment over the garage, Delaney. She would be willing to stay there, to let you two have your privacy.”

Regan finally nodded, reaching for the phone after Tom dialled.

She heard her Mom’s voice, saying hello to Tom. She swallowed hard, trying to work up enough of a volume.

“Mom?”

“Regan? What is going on? Why are you on Tom’s phone? Where is he?”

“He’s right here.” She swallowed against the sobs rising up. “Mom? I need you. Can you come?”

With that, she thrust Tom's phone back at him and turned in Delaney's arms.

Tom could hear Naomi and was finally able to break in, just saying that Regan felt overwhelmed and really just needed her mother. Yes, he agreed, she did. There had been some developments that had changed how Regan was reacting.

Naomi promised to be there as soon as she could. The weather was good and the roads clear. She would be on the way in thirty minutes max, and yes, Riordan would be bringing her.

Regan nodded as Tom touched her shoulder, knowing he needed to talk to her, but she wasn't ready. Not quite yet. He sighed and turned back to study what she had been working on, finally dumping the meat and vegetables into a pot. Stew or soup would work, he thought, and then turned to find the ingredients for biscuits. Delaney and he had worked together many times to put on a meal such as that.

Regan finally turned to him, a small smile creeping across her face as she watched him mixing the dough and then cutting the biscuits.

"Your Mom said she'd leave right away. Your Dad's coming to, I gather. Do you want the rest of them to come?"

"No! I do not! My parents are enough." She sighed. "Although when they hear, they'll come, and put themselves into danger."

"And you don't do that for them?" Delaney had had a long talk with Redmond when he was last there, hearing how Regan had worked to help solve the adventures her brothers had had, even to the point of going in to save them.

Chapter 25

Naomi stared at Delaney as he spoke, Riordan's arm around her shoulder. "You found what?"

"A warning on the garage door. It threatened her life. And we didn't tell you she was kidnapped again, gone for about five hours and then made her way home." Delaney didn't tell them about the bomb in the hallway. He didn't see the need to scare Naomi any further but he knew he would have to tell Riordan. That was a conversation he was not looking forward to.

"Where is she?" Naomi looked around, not seeing Regan or Mick.

"She's sleeping, Naomi. She nodded off when we were eating. She's taken to sleeping back up in her room. Mick won't leave her side. He was with her when she was kidnapped and seems to think she'll disappear on him if he can't see her."

"Bless him. Is it all right if I sneak up and check on her?"

"It is. Second door on your left. At the end of the hall, you'll find another door. That leads to the apartment in the garage. You're welcome to consider it yours to use at any time. That way we all have privacy."

Naomi nodded as she moved away, leaving Riordan staring at Delaney.

"What didn't you say, Delaney?"

"I couldn't tell Naomi that if Regan had gone out of the door where she was kept, she would have triggered a bomb. That bomb would have killed her. She stated to us that she felt God's hand keeping her from even putting a toe out of the door. She managed to escape through a window and flagged down a patrol car."

Riordan nodded. "That sounds about right for Regan. She's recovering. How is her voice?"

"The same. Dad is pushing her to go for more tests but she's digging in her heels. She told me she's afraid. Afraid to find out she'll never heal. But the stress she's under right now? That is affecting her healing. We need this over to get her better."

"And we are working on that, aren't we? Has Tom been around?"

"He has. He knows you're here. He asked if he could drop by in about an hour."

"That works." Riordan's keen eyes studied Delaney. "You're not sleeping either, are you?" He held up a hand. "I know you're not. Remember, I had two sons go through stuff. And theirs was much worse at this point that Regan. That's not to say hers won't worsen, and I would expect that very thing to happen." He looked around as he heard Naomi approaching. "Don't say anything to her yet. I'll be the one to tell her and that's when she's had a chance to settle down somewhat from this."

Naomi reached to hug Delaney, holding on for a bit longer than she would have, before she stood back and studied him. "Delaney, you need to seek your rest." She looked around the kitchen. "I'll take care of this."

Delaney shook his head. "No, I'm not ready to retire. Tom's stopping by in a bit and I really need to start working on my lessons." He gave a laugh. "Like I have anything down yet."

Riordan and Naomi shared a glance before Riordan draped an arm along Delaney's shoulders just as he would his own sons. "Let me help you with that. I'm very good at planning. Or so I'm told."

The two men worked away for a while, Riordan's quiet questions the very impetus that Delaney needed to start making notes. Delaney finally sat back, realizing the time and that he had made a good start on his lesson plans.

"Thank you, Riordan. This has helped enormously. I wouldn't be anywhere close to this without your help." He looked up as he heard a quiet tap at the door. "That would be Tom."

Tom finally rose, shuffling his notes into a tidy pile. Riordan had been a good source of information for him. Together with what Rory had found and what Emma had left him and continued to feed him, he felt confident that they would find the culprits soon. At least, that was his prayer.

Delaney walked out with him, standing for a moment, before he questioned Tom. " ideas on who it is?"

"The detective is still looking into some names. She was amazed by what Emma has been able to feed her. She stated she has never seen such research cross her desk."

Delaney laughed. "That's Emma. She is very thorough. And we had an offer from her husband for a security detail if we needed one."

"Sounds like they are taking care of you. You need to take care of yourself as well, Delaney. You're starting a new chapter in a few weeks and need to be ready for that."

"Riordan worked with me tonight. He's good at asking questions and getting you thinking."

"He always has been able to do that. Listen. I need to run. I have to be away for about a week. A planned vacation I need to go on. I hate leaving when this is going on."

"Take your vacation, Tom. You need it. We'll get by."

"I pray you do. If you need me, call me. I can at least talk to you."

Delaney shook his head. "No, you need a complete break from this."

Tom walked away, not knowing what would happen over the course of the next week, but fear for his friends rising in his heart.

Delaney locked the door, heading up the stairs, knowing Riordan was still at work in his office. He paused at his bedroom door, his head turning towards Regan's room, and then he walked that way, quietly opening the door and slipping through it, to drop to his knees, his head bent in prayer for his young wife. He could feel danger approaching, only he had no idea what or who and because of that, he had no way to prepare. Only God could do that for him.

Chapter 26

Regan watched as her father paced the kitchen, finally getting up and walking away, the back door closing after her. She just couldn't sit there anymore. Mick rubbed against her leg. He barely let her out of his sight and she was grateful for that, but worried that he would be hurt again. She couldn't live with herself if that happened.

She heard the door open and close behind her and sighed even as she stood, staring at the fountain, wanting to see it on but knowing it was too soon. Winter was barely over and it would take a couple of months for it to be warm enough for the water to run freely from the pipes.

"Regan?" Her father's voice sounded behind her. She knew her mother had taken off for the day, heading for Leah's, needing to see her for some reason she hadn't explained.

"Dad? You shouldn't have stayed. You have work you need to be at." She turned, watching him closely. "We need to talk at some point. I don't want to come back. I am more than burned out. I need a real change. Living here in Whitlock is what I need. Delaney is who I need."

"We know, Regan. We know. Your Mom and I have talked about what you may want to do. We realize this is your home. I've been trying to come up with something you could do here remotely but am at a blank. Your Mom is thinking of staring up an online business for her books. She is planning on talking to you about that, to see if you're interested in that."

Regan nodded, a thoughtful look on her face. "It might work. But I need to pray about that and discuss it with Delaney. I don't know what he wants me to do."

"Right now, he wants you safe and to heal. Your voice is not improving."

She shook her head. "Delaney doesn't know that I saw the physician Graeme had recommended. He doesn't know if my voice will ever improve. He held out little hope."

Riordan nodded. "It's not just the volume. It's the damage, isn't it?" He paused. "With that, there is no way you could ever go in again like you were. It's too dangerous." He stared at her for a moment. "I just had a thought. What happens if they have to intubate you at any time"

"It can't happen. The physician thought there would be more damage done if they tried. He's given me this to wear." She held up her arm, a bracelet dangling from it. "It gives information regarding that."

He nodded once more, his attention of a sound he heard. He spun and then shoved at Regan. "Down on the ground, Regan. Now!"

Sounds of shots rang through the air. Delaney paused at the steps and then ran for Riordan and Regan before he spun, his hand going to the side of his head where he had been grazed by a bullet. He hit the ground and laid still.

Blue and red emergency lights flashed through the still afternoon air as men and women in uniform ran for the house and then the backyard, some spreading out to search.

Paramedics following closely, their gear kits in hands, stretchers bumping along the walkway.

Hands reached for Riordan, lifting him slightly to allow Regan to be moved from underneath him. Grave looks were exchanged as they worked feverishly to stem the flow of blood from Riordan's back.

Riordan roused as they worked on him, his eyes on his daughter, fear in his heart as he saw the intubation tube.

"No. Don't do that."

The paramedic spun on his knee, staring at Riordan. "We need to."

"Check her wrist. She has a bracelet. She can't be intubated. She has damage to her throat."

The paramedic froze and then searched for the bracelet, sitting back on his heels as he conversed with his partner. They finally lifted her gently onto a stretcher and almost ran for the ambulance. Riordan followed shortly after. Delaney had already been removed from the area.

Naomi stood at the barricade, hands to her mouth, as she watched the activity before she sought out an officer.

"That's my daughter's home. Her husband and mine are there. What happened?"

The officer shot her a quick look and then spun, beckoning over another officer. A few quick words, and Naomi's arm was gently taken as she was led to a car, tucked inside and then the car sped away for the hospital. The officer simply shook his head when she questioned him, stating he didn't know what all had happened.

Rory and Leah flew through the door to the waiting room, searching for Naomi, who rose when she saw them to be enveloped in Rory's hug.

"Any word yet, Mom?" Rory drew her down, looking up as he heard hurried footsteps and found Reilly and Aideen moving rapidly towards them, Redmond and Ryanne on their heels.

"No. Not yet. They were all shot." She drew in a ragged breath. "I've been able to see Delaney. Graeme took me back. He was grazed by a bullet and they're looking at a possible skull fracture. Your Dad I haven't heard yet. Regan, I had to go in and sign for them to treat her. They wanted to intubate her but they can't."

"They can't, can they? Does she need a ventilator?" Redmond's quiet voice finally broke the silence.

"They haven't said but if she does, they'll do a tracheotomy, they said. I pray they don't have to."

"They are aware of what happened to her?"

"They are. She has somehow acquired a bracelet that gives limited details." She looked up as she heard footsteps and then rose and approached Graeme and Morag.

"Graeme? Morag? Any word of Delaney?"

"No skull fracture. A concussion. He's been awake but can't say much about what happened. He thinks he heard shots and headed outside but other than that he's drawing a blank." Graeme looked behind Naomi at her family. "Any word on Regan or Riordan?"

"Not yet. That makes me afraid of what they're going to say." She looked past him. "And here is the physician. Graeme, can you stay?"

"I can and I will. So will Morag."

The physician eyed Graeme before he nodded. "Mrs. Stuart, I'm the one treating your husband. We need to take him to surgery and soon."

"Why? What is wrong? I didn't think it was that bad."

"It could be. He took a bullet in the back that entered his one lung. We have to go in and repair that damage and then assess for any further damage." He went on to explain the surgery and then handed her the clipboard with the consent.

"What about Regan?"

"Regan?"

"Yes, Regan Callahan. Delaney's wife. That's our daughter."

"Regan? I'm not treating her. Let me see if I can find her physician for you."

Chapter 27

Five hours later, Naomi stood at Riordan's side, her hand on his arm as he moved restlessly. She was fatigued, but refused to leave, not wanting him to awaken without her there. The physicians had tried to make her leave but she just looked at them, bring laughter from her family and the comment that Mom had spoken.

She turned as she heard quiet footsteps and Redmond appeared.

"How is Dad?"

She shrugged. "He hasn't been awake yet. They said the surgery was more extensive than they thought but haven't given all the details yet. They expect him to be in here for a few days." She looked up at her oldest son. "Any word on Regan?"

He shook his head. "Graeme was heading towards where she was, in recovery I think he said, to see if he could find out anything. I'm afraid for her, Mom. This was deliberately done. I talked to the investigator. They were stalked. They found evidence of where someone had laid in wait. Not just one person but two. One on each side of the yard." He paused to compose himself. "What has she gotten mixed up in?"

"I don't know. I'm not sure anyone is clear on that yet." She looked behind her as Graeme quietly entered the room. "Graeme? You have word?"

He drew a deep breath and nodded. "I do. They want you to come and see her, Naomi. Can Redmond stay here for now?"

Redmond nodded, watching as his mother moved away, Graeme's hand under her arm.

Naomi stood for a moment, her eyes on the bed where she knew her daughter lay, lifting them to study the equipment.

"How is her breathing?"

Graeme sighed, knowing what she was asking. "She's on oxygen. The surgeon was able to do the surgery without intubating her or going to a trache tube. That is good news."

"But what is wrong? Where was she hit?"

The surgeon moved towards her as he watched her walk to the bed, her hand coming out to touch her daughter's face.

"Where was she hit, doctor?"

"She was hit in the upper abdomen. She has lost her spleen and a kidney. There was slight damage to the liver which we have addressed."

"That's the total damage? How long will she be in here?"

"A few days, just like your husband." He went on to explain what surgery they had done. "Her husband?"

"He's sleeping, Don, but he'll want to be here as soon as he's able."

The surgeon nodded. "That we can work on but he needs to understand that there will be limits for everyone."

Delaney stood the next day, refusing to sit in the wheelchair used to bring him to Regan's bedside, a hand on her cheek, watching as she slept in the drug induced sleep they had her in. His heart raised in prayer. He had feared she was dead when his father had appeared in his doorway that morning, a grim look on his face. He had felt shattered when he heard that both Riordan and Regan had been shot and the severity of their injuries. His face lifted and grew even grimmer. Somehow he had to find the men responsible and stop this. The next time, someone might well die.

He turned as he felt a presence near him and frowned. He didn't know the man standing there, but when he looked past him, he saw Abe.

"Abe? What are you doing here?"

"We've come to provide protection for you three. Tom heard what happened and had the investigator contact us."

"You can't do this. We can't afford you."

Abe shook his head. "There is no charge. Never is for friends. This is Murphy O'Brien. He's with Regan. I have another one of my team waiting outside for you. His name is Micah."

Delaney finally nodded. "I see. Then you weren't kidding the other night."

"No, I wasn't. Emma's here as well and yes she has our son. Your parents have set us up in the suite in their basement. The guys will take turns being here."

"I guess I can't say anything but thank you, now can I?" He turned back to Regan, finding her the same way as she had been when he turned away.

"How is she?" Murphy's voice was quiet but concerned.

Delaney shrugged. "I have no idea. The surgeon is to be around shortly but Dad said she had extensive internal injuries. And then there's her father."

"Riordan? I was in to see him. He's awake and angry."

"Yeah, well, I would be too, if it was my daughter kidnapped twice, threatened with death more than once, and then shot and left in critical condition."

Murphy and Abe exchanged grim looks before Abe spoke.

"Kidnapped twice? When did this happen?"

"After you were here. She was only gone for about five hours but if she had left through the unlocked door, she would be dead from a bomb. She climbed out a window." He watched his beloved sleep, his hand tracing her cheek. "We even had a death threat painted on our garage door."

Abe nodded, knowing he would be heading out to find the investigator and draw up plans with her. "I have to leave for a while. Call me if you need anything. Murphy can get in touch. Or Micah."

Abe walked away, knowing the difficulty he faced and that his team would be working twelve hour shifts.

A week later, Abe watched as Riordan moved his wheelchair towards his daughter's room for the first time since they had been shot. Delaney walked beside him, a grim look on his face. Abe had talked to Murphy and the word had not been good. They were having trouble in rousing Regan and they could not figure out why.

Murphy watched the two men and then walked towards Abe.

"I know why they can't get her awake." He handed over his phone. "She is very sneaky but I found her injecting what we think was a sedative into Regan's IV. The police have her in custody."

"And she has gotten away with that all week?"

Murphy shook his head. "Just for the last two days. Regan was being weaned off the other medications and should have roused by now. The investigator said she'd be in touch with you." He looked around. "I'm off. Luke is here and in the room."

"Good. Murphy, you did good work today. Thank you."

Murphy nodded and moved away, waving at the family in the waiting room.

Delaney glanced back from the doorway and Abe nodded. He knew they would be talking later, but right now Delaney needed to be with his wife.

Riordan paused just inside the door, his eyes on his daughter before they raised to the younger man standing where he could keep an eye on both Regan and the door. He frowned.

"This is Luke, Riordan. He's one of Abe's men."

"Thank you. We appreciate your being here."

Luke merely nodded, exchanging a glance with Delaney.

Delaney paused at the bedside, his hand finding her face, as she moved restlessly. "Luke? She's rousing?"

Luke moved closer. "She is. Murphy found one of the nurses slipping a sedative into her IV and had her removed."

Riordan looked shocked and then nodded. "That's why she hasn't roused. Who paid her?"

"We don't know. I understand the investigator will be speaking with her and then with you." He moved back, letting them have as much privacy as he could.

Regan's eyes flickered and pain crossed her face as she awoke, her gaze searching the room, taking in the medical equipment, hesitating with fear as she saw Luke, and then finding Delaney's face. Her hand raised to meet his before she saw her father.

"Dad?"

"I'm okay, love. We need to get you well though."

"He won't let us. He's threatened me again. I heard him in this room. Where is he?"

They had to struggle to hear her words. Luke moved closer and then away, his phone out to call Abe. Somehow someone had gotten in and he wanted to know who. There had been restrictions in place.

"Who was here, Regan?"

"A doctor. He was a doctor, Dad. Who is he? Why is he doing this to me?" She looked up at Delaney. "No. No. It wasn't your Dad. I don't know this doctor. Who is he again?" She looked past him as the door opened and the surgeon entered. "That's him. No. I won't see him. Get him away from me."

The surgeon paused, a frown on his face, as Luke moved to stand beside him. "What is she talking about?"

"She has been threatened again, in here, by someone she states is a physician."

"That's impossible. She's been unconscious. There is no way she could have heard that."

"I'm sorry, doctor, but I have to ask you to leave. We will need someone to come in and cover for you, until we get this straightened out."

Delaney watched as the physician shifted on his feet and then straightened his lab coat. He frowned. This was not a physician he knew, and he knew all of them through his father. He caught Luke's eye and shook his head.

Regan caught Delaney's hand. "He's the one. He's the one I heard as well that one day. I heart Baxter and Eric and a female voice and that one. He's the one who drugged me, isn't he?" She could feel the panic rising and tried to quench it.

Delaney gave a sound of dismay, reached for the side rail to lower it and wrapped her in his arms, as much as he could. Riordan watched, a thunderous look on his face.

"There were four, Regan? You've just remembered this?"

She nodded. "I'm sorry. I'm sorry. I'm so sorry, Dad. If I had remembered maybe you wouldn't have been hurt."

"I doubt that, love. They are a well organized bunch. I should mention that we found Eric."

"And what did he have to say?" Delaney wasn't watching Riordan and missed the look of pain on his face. When he didn't answer, Delaney and Regan shared a look before Delaney looked at the older man. "Riordan? What did he have to say?"

"He was dead, Delaney. It looks as if he had been drinking and drove off the road into the lake. They found his car just before Regan asked us to come and stay." He paused, knowing how hard it would be to continue. "They found evidence in there that he had planned to take Regan captive again and move her out of this immediate area. He had rented a cabin up in the middle of the province, near a provincial park."

"I hate to see Tom suffer but I'm glad he's gone. I know. I'm not supposed to think that way. God has the last word and will avenge. I've told myself that over and over. But knowing he's not out there, that helps."

Regan looked around Delaney as the door opened and Luke entered, a slight smile on his face as he found her watching him.

"You're one of Abe's men, aren't you? Which one?"

"Luke."

"And Abigail, isn't it? So if you're here that means all your team is. Where are your wives?"

“They don’t come when we’re on assignment, although I must say they would like this town.”

“Emma’s here, isn’t she?” At his nod, she pointed to the door. “Go. Tell Abe your wives need to be here. Oh, your children. Them too.”

“Not happening, Regan. Not this trip.”

“Then you need to come back and bring them. Delaney wants you to. Mick wants to meet all of you.”

“Mick?” The men watched as Luke tried to determine who Mick was before they began to laugh.

“Mick’s my Border collie, Luke. And yes, I’m sure he would want to meet the team that is keeping his Regan safe.”

“His Regan?”

The men laughed even harder as Regan smirked at him through her pain. “His Regan. He found me in the snow and claimed me. He tolerates Delaney being around me but not so much anyone else.”

“So he’s the one. Why isn’t he in here with you now?”

“That’s what I want to know. Can you clear it for him to come in?”

Luke shook his head as he watched her drift off to sleep, snuggled tight to Delaney. He turned as the door opened and Graeme appeared.

“I hear we have had an issue with a physician.”

“We have, Dad. Now we need someone else to look after her.”

"I know. Phil will be here. You know him well, son. After all he's operated on you a couple of times."

"Don't remind me and don't tell Regan."

"Don't tell Regan what?" Her low voice caught them by surprise and Graeme started to laugh even as Delaney groaned and her father and Luke grinned.

"That your new surgeon operated on me."

"He did? Well then he must be okay." Her voice drifted off as she once more slept, leaving the men staring at her and then one another.

Graeme moved to Riordan's side. "It's time we had you back to your room. Ian I think he said is waiting outside for you."

"Ian it is. Did he mention that he could fly Delaney and Regan somewhere safe where they couldn't be found?"

Luke broke out into hushed laughter as, at their look at him, he explained that Ian had volunteered to fly every lady in trouble somewhere safe but only one had taken him up on the offer.

Chapter 29

A week later, her arms around Delaney's neck as he carried her up the stairs to their home, Regan sighed. She was home but it wouldn't make any difference. She still couldn't do much. She was under strict orders that way. She knew Delaney was worried. His classes were to start in a couple of days and he had been back and forth to the college. He didn't want to leave her alone but he had no choice.

Abe had had his team go through their home and the workshop, tightening up their security, but Regan knew it wouldn't matter. If someone wanted to get to her, they could. She would be long gone before any response came.

Delaney watched her face for pain and then headed for her favourite room. He set her on her feet and then gently shoved her to the couch, sitting beside her.

"I'm glad I'm home, Delaney. I just wish this was over."

"I do too. Tom has asked if he could drop by later. He'll call first. I told him it depended how you were." He sighed. "He wants to bring the new investigator with him, to update us on the progress of the case."

"Is that what we are, Delaney? Just a case?"

"Not to Tom. Or to any of our people here. I know for a fact they're working on it, on their own time."

"They shouldn't."

"It's how our town works, Regan. Now, can I get you anything?"

She shook her head. "I'm okay for now. You need to work on your stuff for your classes."

He grinned at her. "Then that's what I'll do, go work on my stuff. Call me if you need me. Or send Mick. He's good at finding people."

Regan rubbed at Mick's head on her knee. "He is at that. Thank you, Delaney."

Later that afternoon, Delaney stood back from the door, reaching to shake Tom's hand and then the woman's hand who was with him.

"Delaney, this is Angela Murray. She's the investigator who has Regan's case. Is Regan up?"

Delaney hung their coats up and then pointed towards the conservatory. "In her favourite room. You know the way. I'll be right in. Just watch for Mick. He's become very protective of her. I'm the only one he lets near her. Not even Mom or Dad can get close."

Angela stared at him. "And just who is Mick?"

Delaney grinned. "My dog."

She shook her head. "I've heard of that, but never seen it. This will be interesting. And how do they keep getting to her if that's the case?"

"The first time he found her. The next time, they took him out. And the last time, they were farther away and he couldn't protect her from the bullets. Does that explain it?" Delaney had to hold back his frustration at her comments.

Tom stood for a moment in the doorway, watching Regan, not quite sure how to approach her, knowing that his brother had planned to kidnap her again.

Regan heard the low growl from Mick and looked up, a smile on her face as she saw Tom.

"Tom. You're back from your holiday. Did you relax at all?"

Tom grinned as he sat at the other end of the couch, his eyes on Mick for a moment until the dog's attention moved to Angela. "I did. I needed it. That cabin I found up north is wonderful. I can give you and Delaney the information and when this is all over, you two can head up there."

"That sounds wonderful, Tom. I'm sorry about your brother."

He blinked. "Thank you. I know that's not how I expected you to respond."

"Then, you don't know me. He was your brother and you loved him. I know I should be bitter and angry but God dealt with him."

"That he did, Regan. I just don't know where he was in that walk."

"You won't know, not likely." Her eyes shifted to Angela, who had taken a seat across from her. "And who do we have here?"

"I'm Detective Angela Murray. I'm the one working your case. It's interesting to say the least."

Regan grinned at her. "It would be. This is nothing compared to what my two brothers went through."

Angela stared at her. "Brothers? Why? What happened to them?" Her eyes grew round as Regan explained what had transpired with Rory and Reilly.

When she could straighten out her thoughts and the information she had just been thrown, Angela drew a deep breath. "I must say you have an interesting family. And an interesting career."

"Not . Dad has accepted my resignation from the company. Right now, I'm at loose ends." She looked up as Delaney shifted her over on the couch and sat beside her.

Delaney shared a look with Tom before speaking. "Detective, you have word?"

"Not what I wanted." She sipped at the mug of tea she had been handed. "There is a lot of background information we're sorting through. And someone named Emma keeps sending me more. Do you know anything about that?"

Delaney looked down at Regan as she grinned. "I do. Have you heard of Trackers?"

Angela blinked. "Who hasn't in the law enforcement field. Whoever that is they're good." She paused, seeing the smiles on the younger couple's faces and groaned. "No, don't tell me. Emma is Tracker?"

"She is. Anything she sends you will have been verified and proven. She's on contract with a number of forces to provide just such research to them."

"Then we need to get her on board with us. The material is wonderful. It has saved a lot of time on our part. I wonder why we've never used her before."

"Because she is very selective as to what work she takes on. The only reason she has with us is that we're friends and have been for years." Regan looked up at Delaney as the doorbell rang. "Were we expecting anyone else tonight? I hoped we weren't." Fatigue lined her face as she leaned against him.

Tom rose. "Let me go."

They heard voices and looked up at the sound of footsteps. Emma and Abe appeared in the doorway, to their surprise.

"Emma? Abe? What are you two doing here? You just went home two days ago. Don't tell me. Ian's here to fly Regan somewhere safe." Delaney rose to hug Emma and shake Abe's hand.

"That he has volunteered to do. He says he knows of a few places here in the province he could use. She wouldn't be found." Abe's attention shifted to Angela. "Angela Murray. It has been a number of years."

Angela stared at him. "Abe Finlay? You're the Abe they mentioned? I never knew that. I have been trying to find you to thank you for protecting that witness for us."

Abe shrugged. "That's what we do. Rebel's Security, if you need us."

Angela's attention turned to Emma. "And this is Emma?"

"That would be me." Emma reached to shake her hand. "Now, where were you in your discussion?"

"To tell you the truth, they had just talked about you two and you walked in." Angela shook her head. "I don't know how you did that."

"God. God knew we needed them here. Emma has more information, I would hazard a guess." Delaney knew they wouldn't have come unless it was important. "Emma?"

She shared a glance with Abe and then Tom before she turned to Delaney and Regan. "We do have information and that we felt we needed to give to you in person."

Chapter 30

Regan finally looked up, fatigue weighing her down. Delaney took one look at her and then stood, sweeping her into his arms, and excusing them from the room. He set her down on her bed, his eyes on her.

"Regan? Do you need anything? I have your pain meds here. You need to take some."

She nodded. "Let me take them and then I'll just lie down for a while. I need to hear what they're saying."

Delaney covered her with a blanket before he stood, eyes thoughtful and then turned for the door, leaving on a low light. He smiled as he saw Mick standing outside the door.

"Go on in, Mick. She needs you, even though she's asleep."

Delaney stood for a moment outside the conservatory door, trying to compose himself. He could hear Tom and Emma discussing the case, with comments from Angela. He prayed that they could solve this before Regan was hurt any further, but he doubted that would happen. He slipped back in and to his seat, Abe's eyes on him.

Angela finally looked up from her notes, her eyes thoughtful. "Where would you head next, then, Emma, if you were researching more?"

"That I can't answer. I don't know where you are heading, who your suspects are, things like that. If you have names, shoot them off to me and I'll look into it. I don't want to see this go cold. I've seen that too many times and then something happens. That usually is not good. I've seen too many people die because a little bit of information was missed, or overlooked, or not available. I would talk to all of Regan's family. I know her father is just recovering but when I spoke with him earlier today, he is adamant he will not sit by and see her hurt again."

"I understand." Angela shared a look with Tom. "One thing that I don't understand. This shooting? It was overboard for what Regan has been facing. How sure, Tom, are you that she was the target?"

Tom nodded. "I know where you're heading, Angela. We had the same thoughts. We have asked Rory or Redmond to go through their files and see if there was ever a threat made against Riordan. It almost seems as if he was the target with the shooting, not Regan. Regan they seem to want to keep alive. This was a deliberate attempt at assassination."

Delaney sat back, his thoughts in a turmoil. He had wondered at the shooting, but hadn't realized that where the investigation was heading. "So you're saying we have different groups involved? And they are after Regan because of her Dad? But that doesn't explain what had happened to her."

"No, it doesn't. Tom, what were your thoughts on that?" Angela looked down at her notes, feeling that she was missing something vital and not sure what.

"You need to find the woman at the top. And it will be a woman. This with Regan? It feels like vengeance and jealous, more so than anything else. Delaney has gone over everything he can think of and doesn't know who she is. The name we were given was a false one and led nowhere."

Delaney nodded. "I have written out every name I can think of - male or female. Team members. Students. Volunteers. Security. There was quite a list. Angela, I think it was sent on to you."

"It was? I don't remember seeing it and I should have."

Tom sighed. "I sent it by courier the day I left. There should be a record of it being delivered." He reached for his phone, pulling up his email. "It says it was delivered. Let me have your email, Angela, and I'll send the information to you. I have a copy at home I can hand deliver tomorrow."

Delaney was on his feet and quickly out of the room and back, a sheaf of papers in his hands. "Here. This is a copy of what Tom had. I keep copies of everything I do."

"Thank you, Delaney. This will help. Will you be around the next day or so if I need to talk?"

"I will be but classes start soon and that takes up my days, but if we need to, we can work around the schedule. Regan will be here during the day if you need to speak with her. Just watch Mick, that's all I ask."

"We can do that. Tom?"

"We'll talk more, Delaney. We're off. Don't get up." Tom and Angela walked out, Delaney watching them before he turned to Abe and Emma.

"There's more to you two being here." Delaney watched the couple exchange glances.

"We are, Delaney. Micah was concerned enough he had his wife, Kat, start looking into family trees for the ones we suspect, namely Eric, Baxter, the last trip Regan was on. In case you didn't know, Kat can trace back family trees. She's written programs just for that. Her preliminary work had her worried enough she tracked me down at midnight last night."

"And why would she be so concerned?" Delaney was puzzled.

"Tom. She's not sure about him. Eric was not his brother, did you know that? He was a cousin his parents took in and raised, never telling either one that they weren't siblings."

"And this comes out now. This will hurt Tom." Delaney rubbed at his face, unsure what to ask. "I'm not sure where this is going."

"We're still working through that. Micah has pulled himself off the team for now to work with Kat and Emma. Jace and Naomi is her office are working on it when they can. This has become a priority for them." Abe watched as Delaney drew a deep breath. "And before you ask, there is no charge. We've told you that. We don't charge friends, and that's what you two are."

Emma handed over a folder. "This is the information we have so far. I would ask that you not talk to Tom about this. It needs to come from an official standing. I don't like what I'm finding. There is so much hidden, and we can't tie it to Regan. Not yet. Before you ask, your family and hers have been looked at. That surgeon? He was not the one she thought it was. He's in the clear. He's upset that she thought that of him but he understood."

"Then who did she hear? She wouldn't have said that if she hadn't been sure she had."

"We're going back over everyone that had access to the room. Given that one of my men were in there the whole time, it's interesting, to say the least. We're looking at the nurses now. One of her nurses was a male and we're having trouble finding a history of him. Do you know Dom Porter?"

Delaney's hand froze as he was raising his mug to his hand. "I do, and it's not good. He was a troublemaker through school. We always suspected he was behind a lot of the vandalism in town, but no one could catch him. Is he involved?"

"It would appear he is. Jace is tracking down more on him, but if you have anything, any names, that is connected to him, please let me know."

A grim look on his face, Delaney reached for a pad of paper and a pen, quickly writing down names, dates, circumstances, how he knew Dom, before he tore off the pages and handed them to Emma. "Here. This should help. I haven't seen him in town, but he could have been." His voice died away and his eyes slid closed. "Look at the security people on the last dig. I thought one of them looked like him but he made sure I didn't get close to him. That would explain the photos that have shown up."

"This will help. Thank you, Delaney." Emma looked at him, compassion on her face. "How is Regan?"

"She's hurting and won't admit it. She wants to work on finding the people responsible and doesn't like it that she can't. She's upset that her father was shot, but not knowing which one they were after doesn't help."

"If we can do anything more for you, please call us. We mean that. If we have to, Ian will fly you two away somewhere, but somehow I doubt that would help." Abe looked at Emma who nodded. "If you do need to get away for a few days, let us know. You're welcome to come and stay at our place."

"Thank you, Abe, Emma. That means a lot, but with classes starting soon and it being my first teaching stint, we need to stay here. If necessary, I'll send Regan your way."

Delaney stood with his hand against the door, his head down, his body sagging with worry and fatigue. He finally moved through the house, checking locks and turning off lights. He stood, his hand on the handrail, before he trudged up the stairs, almost too tired to lift a foot to reach the next step. He stood for a moment at the top of the stairs, finally heading to check on Regan. He stood beside her, seeing the tears that had tracked down her face, tears of pain, he knew, but tears of what else, he wasn't sure. All he knew was that the woman he loved and adored was hurting and he just couldn't make it better. Lord, I have no words to pray, but You know my heart. Your will, Lord, is what I pray.

He sank down beside her, pulling a blanket over him, reaching to encircle her with his arms, pulling her tight to him, watching Mick as he stood for a moment beside the bed before he jumped up, to curl up beside Regan.

Chapter 31

A month later, healed from her physical wounds, but still afraid and trying not to let anyone know, Regan paced her home. Delaney was due home from the college at any time and she so wanted to see him but was unsure if he could even help her. Arms wrapped around herself, she stopped at the kitchen table, staring at the box she had brought in with the mail, but there was no postmark on it. That fact frightened her.

She spun around and headed for the entryway as she heard a key in the lock. Delaney saw her coming towards him as he closed the door, dropped his briefcase and just enveloped her close to his heart, standing for a while before he looked down at her.

"Regan?"

She stepped back, her eyes looking everywhere but at him. "How was your day?"

"It was okay. The students are settling down into their work and so is their professor." He looked past her at Mick standing in the kitchen doorway. "Regan? What happened today? I don't see the confident woman I have come to expect meeting me at the door. You have been so much like the Regan from before I keep forgetting what we're in the midst of."

She turned, her throat closing for a moment as she tried to articulate. Her voice had not healed that much and she had come to accept that's how it would be.

"A parcel came today, Delaney. There's no postmark on it, though."

“Where is it?” A grim look crossed his face.

“In the kitchen. I tried to call Tom but only got his voice mail. I wasn’t sure if we should call Angela or not.”

He stood, his arms around Regan, as he studied the parcel, not moving it. “You just carried it in, right?”

“That’s right. I would have left it outside if I had known what it looked like.”

He nodded, his eyes on her face. “Let me try Tom again. If not him, then I will call Angela.” He turned as he heard the doorbell. “Were we expecting someone?”

“No, we weren’t. We were to be going out for dinner.” She sighed, knowing their night had just changed.

She heard Delaney and then Tom as they walked back through the house. She greeted Tom and then pointed at the table. “Please? Get that out of here.

“Good evening to you too, Regan. What do we have here?”

“I have no idea. And I don’t think I want to know.” She turned and walked away, Mick at her heels.

Tom watched her leave before he turned to Delaney. “Delaney, what happened?”

He pointed at the table. “She found that. I would say she’s been pacing since this morning, not wanting to disturb me at college. She did say she tried to call you but your phone went straight to voice mail.”

"That's odd. I've gotten every other call today." He checked his phone. "There's no call coming from her and that is odd."

"It is odd. Regan has your number programmed in and that's what she would have used. Let me get her phone." Delaney was back, Regan's phone in hand, as he scrolled through her calls. "Here is it. And it is your number. What is going on, Tom?"

"Can I borrow her phone for a day or so? I would like our techs to take a look at it. It's as if my number is blocked somehow. And that is very odd." He turned to the parcel. "I'll take that as well."

"Tom, wait." Delaney had a hand on Tom's arm. "You stopped by tonight. Why?"

Tom shrugged. "I felt I had to and I guess this is why. I hadn't talked to you two in a couple of days and just wanted to make sure you were fine."

"We're fine, Tom. Now, what are you going to do about that?" Regan's low voice had the men turning to look at her, a grin coming across Tom's face.

Tom shook his head. "I'm taking it with me and turning it over to the lab. They'll go over it with a fine tooth comb as they say." He walked away, leaving them staring after him before they moved to the door.

A sudden explosion rocked the night and Delaney threw himself over Regan as they lost their footing and landed on the floor. He looked up and then was out the door, calling for Regan to call for help. He stood, staring at Tom's car for a moment as flames from it lit up the night before he began calling for hm, searching the area, praying Tom was not in the vehicle. His foot caught on something and he tumbled to the ground, rolling and staring behind him before he was on his knees, his hands reaching for Tom.

Regan stood for a moment, shock coursing through her, before she too was on her knees.

"Is he alive, Delaney?"

"He is. He's hurt, but he's alive. What happened?" Delaney stood and moved back from Tom as emergency personnel descended on the area, reaching to pull Regan back with him.

"The parcel? Where is it?" Regan frantically began to look for it.

"We'll tell the officers and they can search. Back up on the porch, Regan. They'll want to talk to us."

She finally nodded, sinking down into one of the white wicker chairs she had placed on the porch earlier that day, finding the weather warm enough for her to do that.

The young couple finally shut the door behind them and just stood, their eyes on one another, seeing the shock and fear they were both feeling at that point.

"Was it the parcel, do you think, Delaney?"

He nodded. "I'm thinking it was. It was likely set on a timer, with whoever sent it thinking we would be at home and that they would hit us. But who?" He sighed as he heard the doorbell. "I was hoping we were done for the night."

He pulled open the door, to find Angela standing there. "Angela. What can we do for you?"

She stepped inside. "I just heard. How is he?"

Delaney shrugged. "I have no idea. They wouldn't tell me. You likely will be able to find out more than we can."

She nodded, her glance shifting between them. "I was heading here anyway, just to give an update, but this isn't a good time. Someone said he had taken a parcel from here?"

"He had and I have no idea what was in it. Excuse me, Angela. This is not a good time for me." Regan turned and walked up the stairs, not looking back.

Delaney followed her with his eyes before he turned back to Angela. "Come on out to the kitchen. Can I get you anything?"

She shook her head. "I really need to talk with Regan. But I'll come back. We need to talk in the next couple of days. I want to update her on the investigation."

"This is Monday. Thursday or Friday is best. This will take her time to come back from." Delaney stood in the kitchen, hearing Angela close the door behind her before he headed to it and locked it, turning to find Regan at the bottom of the stairs.

"Regan?"

She just shook her head and tried to speak, but no words could be heard.

"Regan? What happened?"

She shrugged, tears on her cheeks, as she stared at him before she could speak, her voice barely audible. "I don't know, Delaney. I'm just such a danger to everyone."

"I don't think so. Today was a set up of some kind. Tom never got a call from you."

"And I called him, more than once. He took my phone.   Now we will never know what happened."

Delaney wrapped her in his arms. "No, we not likely will. Now that our date night is off, what can we get for supper?"

She shoved at him. "Supper?"

"Yes, supper. We need to eat, at least I do."

She just shook her head and turned away from him. "I left sandwiches in the fridge earlier, thinking we could go on a picnic. I'm heading for bed."

Delaney's head dropped.   Lord, this is not what I wanted to happen. She's finding it so hard to trust You. I can see it. I can hear it. You are the only one who can reach her. None of the rest of us can. And now I have to call Dad and then Riordan and let them know what just happened.

Chapter 32

Delaney turned the next day, hearing his name called and frowning. He didn't know the man running towards him but he seemed to know him.

"Excuse me? Do I know you?"

The man grinned and shook his head. "No, we've never met. I'm Abe's brother-in-law, Gideon. Abe asked me to track you down. I was heading this way anyway for something else."

"Gideon? The private investigator? Abe mentioned you but I didn't know you did work for him."

"Every once in a while I get called in. Is there somewhere we can talk?"

Delaney looked around and then pointed towards a park bench. "Will that work? I'm done for the day. Or I can take you to my place and set Regan loose on you." He grinned as Gideon stared at him for a moment.

"No, we don't want to talk to Regan. At least not yet. That may come."

"So, what the deep dark secret then?"

Gideon shook his head. "That's what it is, Delaney. We heard about Tom. That was planned. It had nothing to do with Regan. It was just coincidental it was at your place. At least that's what we've heard."

"And how would you hear that if you're not from here?"

"We have our sources and those are trusted sources. That parcel I understand Regan received.

Did you know they found it last night?   It was intact."

"We thought it had been destroyed in Tom's car. Does that mean her phone is intact as well?"

Gideon nodded. "It is. Angela has it and the parcel. She took over that investigation as well as it all seemed to relate to what you two are going through."

'But you don't think so."

Gideon looked down for a few moments, sorting through his thoughts. "No, we don't. I had a long talk with both Abe and Emma and then the police chief in our town, who is a good friend of ours. None of us are convinced that Regan was a target. If she had been, that parcel would have detonated when it was in your house. Angela will be in touch, she said, to talk to you two."

"She was there last night. I told her not before Thursday at the earliest. Last night took a lot from Regan."   Delaney paused, composing himself. "When she came back down after Angela left, she couldn't talk. Whatever it is that affecting her? The fear last night drove her ability to articulate away."

"That's interesting. You said your father had her assessed?"

"He did." Delaney paused, his eyes catching a look on Gideon's face. "What is it?"

"Has she been taking any medication for it?"

Delaney paused in his movements, his hand rubbing at the back of his neck. "How did you know?"

Gideon shrugged. "Just a guess. A physician friend once told me about a street level drug that can be used like this. Where has she been getting her medication from?”

“Our local pharmacy.” Delaney sat back abruptly. “And that pharmacy has been under investigation lately for drug dealing.” He rose, his hand catching at Gideon’s arm. “You’re coming with me. Where’s your vehicle?”

“Right near yours, I think. I’ll follow you.”

Regan stared at Delaney as he asked where her medication was. “Why? I’m taking it as I should.”

“Gideon here would like to take a sample with him. He thinks that’s what causing your loss of voice.”

“And how would that happen? Aren’t we getting it from the pharmacy?”

“We are, and I heard today the pharmacy’s under investigation for drug dealing. We need to have your medication assessed by someone outside of town. Gideon has offered to do just that.”

Regan stared at Delaney and then past him at Gideon before she spun, her hand reaching for the medication bottle that she slapped into Delaney’s hand.

“Find out. I want to know what it is. If that’s what has caused this, I want to know who and why.”

“We’ll find out. Dad sent you to that physician. We’ll look into him.”

She shook her head. "I haven’t seen him in months. He had given me enough refills on that prescription that I haven’t had to go back.” She pointed towards the medication bottle. “Is that what’s been behind how I’ve been feeling? You know well I’m not myself.” Tears filled her eyes that she fiercely blinked to control. She turned to Gideon. "You said Abe sent you?"

"He did, Regan. He's that concerned. And when Abe is that concerned, he takes steps." He grinned suddenly. "At least, he didn't sent Ian."

"And that is good news because?" Regan was puzzled for a moment, feeling Delaney's arms come around her as his body shook with laughter.

"Because, my love, Ian is known for offering to fly the ladies in danger to safety."

"He is? Maybe that's what we should do." She sighed. "Only you can't. You have your classes."

Gideon studied them, seeing the stress they were under. "How be I talk to Abe and Ian and find a spot you two can get away to for a bit. Delaney, I understand your college has a reading week coming up in two weeks?"

"They do. Now, why didn't I think of that? I can make arrangements not to be around. I have been assured that if I need to take Regan away somewhere, my classes would be covered. I have done up lessons and video series for on line courses and they would use those."

Gideon nodded. "Let me work on that. You two need to get away." He waved the medication bottle. "I think once you're off these, you'll be fine, Regan. It may take a bit of time and I am afraid you might go through withdrawal."

She shook her head. "I have been taking them, but they don't seem to be working. Is that why? It's not the right medication?"

Gideon squinted at the name of the drug. "No, I don't think this is. This is for mood swings and depression. Somehow I don't think that diagnosis would be what caused your voice loss. I know this medication. It does have side effects but not that severe. Unless they've dispensed this under that name and it's a substitute drug."

Regan paused in her movements, before she shoved at Delaney's arms. She ran from the room and then back, papers in her hands. "Here. This is what I found out. I was going to talk to Delaney tonight. The pharmacist always said he had to dispense the drugs. He wouldn't let one of the assistants do it."

Gideon scanned the papers, alarmed at what she had found. "How did you find this information on him?"

"It wasn't real hard. It's out there. All I did was put in his name." She leaned against Delaney as he wrapped an arm around her. "Has he been the one all along? Not the surgeon?"

"That we are working on. I know Angela is as well." He glanced at his watch. "I need to run but one of us will be in touch with you."

Chapter 33

Two weeks later, Regan stood in a remote cabin, staring around at the interior before she walked back out the door and headed for the lake the cabin was situated on. She watched as Ian took off in the float plane he had borrowed. He had promised to be back in seven days but they could call him if they needed to go home before that. He assured them there was cell reception. She wouldn't know, she thought. She had not bothered to replace her phone, even though Delaney had pressed her to do just that. If she needed to talk to one of her family, she borrowed his.

Delaney watched from the dock as Regan made her way towards him, reaching to hug her.

"Okay, my love?"

She shrugged. "I have no idea, Delaney. I know my voice is back, my mood swings had disappeared, Dad is healing, the rest of the family is safe, but I feel that we have a huge cloud over us, just ready to drop a torrent of danger."

"That's a good way to describe it. Now, that we're here, we'll have time to help you heal."

"I need this time, Delaney. I need to reconnect with God. We need this time." She turned in his arms, watching the sun set over the lake. "Did Abe say how he found this place?"

"He refused to tell me, just that he knew the owner."

A week later, Ian stared around the area. There were no signs of Delaney or Regan. He searched the cabin, finding their belongings but not them. They had agreed on the date and time. He knew they wouldn't have disappeared on their own, not with the plans they had made. He sighed, pulling out his phone.

"Abe?"

"Ian? Why are you calling?"

"They're gone, Abe. I can't find them. They're not here. And by the looks of it, haven't been in a couple of days."

Ian could hear Abe's sharply indrawn breath. "No sign of them? Stay put. I'm making some calls. And we're heading that way."

Ian pocketed his phone, his eyes on the ground. It had rained the night before, washing away any signs around the cabin. He widened his search, finally stopping at a trail opposite the lake, seeing signs of footprints. Delaney's and Regan's, he thought, but there are more than theirs. Lord, protect them.

Abe stood beside Ian three hours later, watching the movement of the police. "No sign?"

"Just where I could see them heading into the bush. They weren't alone, Abe. That's a given. They didn't leave freely."

"No, they didn't. I just wonder how they were found. We were too careful."

"I know. There were only three people in their area who knew where they were heading."

Ian nodded. "How deep is Emma searching?"

"Deep. She has made a connection with Regan that I don't often see. She's worried about her and Delaney."

"I'm sure she is."

Three days later, Graeme turned from Delaney's front door as he heard his name called. Tom walked towards him.

"Tom? How are you?"

Tom shrugged. "I've been better. How are Delaney and Regan? I heard they had taken off for a week."

"That's the thing, Tom. No one has seen them since Ian dropped them off at the cabin. When he went to bring them out, they were gone."

Tom's face went white. "They've disappeared. Angela never said a word when I talked to her earlier. And she knew. She knew we're involved in their protection here. How could she not say anything?"

"That's something we all want to know. She was one of only three people who knew where they were going. Abe arranged it. Ian flew them in."

Tom stared at his friend and then nodded. "I get what you're not saying. Have you been into the house?"

"I was just heading that way. We have Mick at our place, and he's been restless. Has been for days now." Graeme paused, counting the days, and groaned. "That would have been about the time they disappeared. How did he know?"

Tom shrugged. "Some dogs just have that connection with their owners that even when they are miles apart, they can tell if something's wrong. Don't beat yourself up, Graeme. You wouldn't or couldn't have known."

"No, but it doesn't make it any easier to bear, now does it?" Graeme shoved open the door and stopped short. "We're not going any further, Tom."

"Why?" Tom peered over Graeme's shoulders. "I see what you mean. Back out, Graeme. Close the door. I'll bring in a team."

Tom walked towards Graeme and Riordan a few hours later. He had called Riordan, asking that he come to Whitlock. A grim look covered his face. The team had found evidence that Delaney and Regan had been back there in the last couple of days, but they hadn't been on their own. That much was evident.

"Tom?" Riordan's voice caught his attention.

"They've been here, Riordan, but someone was with them. We don't know if anything is missing. Graeme, I'll have an officer walk you through as you likely know the house the best of the two of you."

Graeme nodded. "What about the workshop?"

"We're processing that now." Tom winced as he moved wrong, still suffering with pain from his injuries. "We'll need you to go through that too."

Chapter 34

Delaney paced the room he and Regan were in, trying once more to find a way out. He needed to get her out and hadn't found that way yet. He studied her, seeing the whiteness of her face, but also the resolve there that she wouldn't be a victim again. He had no idea who had taken them. The men had appeared abruptly on their fifth day at the cabin, forcing them away and through the woods to a vehicle they were almost thrown into.

Regan watched from where she stood, leaning against the wall, her arms crossed over her abdomen. She was puzzled about this whole scenario, she thought. They had been taken from the cabin, forced to ride miles to their home, forced into their home as it was searched. She snorted. Tossed is how the police would describe it, she knew. Then they were forced to the vehicle again and brought here. No words had been exchanged with them or among the men and she found that strange. She finally shoved away from the wall and headed towards the window. Once more, she was on the main floor. Her fingers felt along the window frame and then reached for the lock, surprised to find she could turn it.

Delaney stopped behind her, watching closely as Regan pushed at the window, seeing it raise under her hands. He shook his head at her and then peered out, not seeing anyone but recognizing the area. They were on the edge of town, close to their home in fact. He was puzzled. This just seems so off, he thought.

He dropped out of the window, reaching to help Regan, before grasping her hand and running for the trees close to them. He watched behind them, not seeing any activity. He frowned. He hadn't heard any activity, now that he thought of it, for the last day or so. He knew they hadn't been brought any food or water and that made him wonder what was up.

Regan tugged at his hand, pointing towards their home. He shook his head, moving away from there. He finally stopped, eyes watchful, as Regan leaned against him.

"Delaney? You're not taking us home?"

He shook his head. "That's where they will be. Watching for us. Mom and Dad's place is not far. Are you up for a bit more of a walk?"

"I am. Just as long as we don't bring danger to them."

"I think we already have. This is bizarre, you know."

"I know. That's what puzzling me. What were they looking for that they didn't find?"

"I have no idea. And I have no idea how they found us. I know it wasn't Ian or Abe."

"No. Angela?" She shook her head. "I don't get it and I'm not sure I ever will."

Hand in hand, they walked forward, stopping at the edge of the backyard to Graeme's home.

"Can we just walk in?" Regan looked around, not sure what she was looking for. This was too reminiscent of her trips to bring women out.

"We should be able to." He glanced at his watch. "Dad will be up."

"Did we really just walk away from there? Where were they?"

"I'm not sure. I didn't feel like we were watched." He moved her quickly to the back of the house, reaching for the door knob and finding it turning under his hand. "This is strange. Dad never leaves the door unlocked this early."

Regan dropped to her knees, wrapping Mick in a hug, his tongue moving rapidly as he swept it across her face. "Mick never alerted. How come?"

Graeme stood watching them. "He knew you were out there. He came to find me. That's why the door was unlocked, son."

"Thanks, Dad. Where's Mom?"

"Behind you, son."

Delaney spun as his mother wrapped him into a hug before moving to hug Regan. She stood, arm around the younger woman, as she searched her son's face.

"I have no idea how you got here or where you've been. I'm just glad you're here." She looked past Graeme as she heard more footsteps. "Your father's here, Regan. And so is Tom."

"They are? How did they know to be here?"

"We've been working all night, trying to think of how to find you. Instead you walked right in." Riordan pulled his daughter into a tight hug, not wanting to let her go, and then reached to hug Delaney.

"Sit, all of you. I'll make us something to eat while these two tell us their adventures."

Delaney and Regan shared a look as they sat before Regan spoke.

"I'm not sure what to say. The men never spoke. They pulled us from the cabin, took us to the house while they searched it and then stuffed us in a house near our own home. They disappeared yesterday and we didn't see them as we just opened a window and walked away."

Delaney grinned at her concise description. "That's about what happened. We didn't see any faces. All we can give are generalized descriptions of them. Nothing stood out. Not on them. Not on their clothing. Not on the vehicle."

Regan finally looked at Tom before she spoke. "Tom? What are your thoughts?"

He shrugged, even as he thanked God that her voice was normal. "I'm not sure what to think, Regan. It's strange. That's twice you've been able just to walk away."

"I know. It's like they let me. Let us." She glanced at Delaney. "Why would they do that?"

"That's something we'll ask them when we find them. Any impressions, feelings, whatever, let me know."

"How did they find us?"

"That's something Abe is working on. He hasn't said who he suspects."

"He suspects Angela. There's been something off about her all along." Regan grew angry, surprising them all but her father. "She's been using us and I want to know why. Please, don't let her know where we are. Just that we're safe. Delaney needs to go back to his classes, I know that. How do we do this?"

Chapter 35

Standing on her front porch, Regan stared down Angela, knowing that the investigation no longer rested in her hands.

"Why did you did that, Regan? Why ask for another investigator?" Angela was angry and trying to control that.

"Because it's going nowhere. Because someone found us. I don't know that I or Delaney can trust you anymore. Please, leave." Regan turned, walked into the house, and closed and locked the door, watching through a window as Angela finally left.

She turned, not feeling safe in her house, and ran for her purse, grabbing Mick's leash and running for her car. She headed away from home, not too sure where she would end up, but knowing she needed to be around someone. She finally parked at the college, and with Mick's leash in hand, headed for Delaney's office. They had been there before, these two, and were known to the staff. She slumped in a chair in his office, knowing he would find her when he could.

Delaney stood for a moment, eying the open door to his office before he moved close enough to spot Regan and Mick. He sighed. Something had spooked her, he was sure, and she had run from home, ran to him. He glanced at his watch. He was done for the day, with classes anyway. He would just lock up and take her home.

Mick raised his head as he spied Delaney, his tail moving in greeting. Regan looked up and then was on her feet, her arms tight around Delaney, sobs shaking her body. That concerned him. He knew she seldom wept, was more apt to walk away and compose herself. He stood, just holding her, trying to convey to her that she was safe, but not sure if he had.

"Regan? What happened?"

"Angela happened." He heard the anger in her voice. "She showed up and confronted me. Wanted to know why she was off the case."

"And what did you tell her?"

"Just that we asked for someone new, that the case wasn't moving."

"And she grew angry. But that wouldn't have made you run."

"No, it wasn't all that happened. I was getting hang up calls every five minutes. Text messages with gravestones. Mick sensed someone around the house. I couldn't stay there. I needed to see you."

"I'm glad you came to me. Let me lock up and we'll head home."

"No, not home. Let Tom go through first, please? Let's go find him."

Tom looked up from his paperwork as the desk officer tapped at his door and then entered.

"Tom, Delaney and Regan are here. She's looking rattled, if you get my drift."

"They are? She is? Let's get them back here." Tom was on his feet, moving towards the front desk, pausing as he watched Delaney and Regan. Something's happened, he thought, and it's been enough to shake Regan.

"Delaney. Regan. Come with me." Tom led them to a conference room, closing the door and pointing to chairs. "Sit. Now. What brings you here?"

"Angela for one thing." Delaney watched Regan's face, seeing the fear she was trying to hide. "She showed up today at our place. She shouldn't have. She was removed from the case. You have it again, I believe, Tom."

"I do. And you're right. She should not have come to see you. She have talked to me." Tom leaned against the table, his eyes thoughtful. "What all did she say?"

"Not much, Tom. It was just so bizarre. It's like she was fishing for information, information I didn't give her."

He nodded. "I'll talk to her and let her know she has to stay away. It's not her investigation now and she can't interfere. If I need to, I'll go to her supervisor." He studied the two. "But what else?"

Regan handed over her phone. "Hang up calls. Texts with gravestones. That's been going on all day." She frowned. "That was until I took Mick and found Delaney. We dropped my vehicle and Mick off at home before we came to find you."

Tom studied her phone, scrolling through the call log and then her text messages, a frown appearing on his face. "They're from an unknown number, blocked call. I can turn this over to the lab but I'm not sure how far we can get."

"That's what I suspected." Regan reached for her phone. "Who is doing this, Tom? How do we stop them?"

"We don't want to go public, give a news conference. Given your family's line of work, that would expose what they do, and we don't want that. Let me think this through."

Regan was on her feet, at the door, before she spun. "Think it through all you like, Tom. I have had enough."

Delaney shrugged as Tom eyed him. "What she said. Call us later, please? At least, let us know where the investigation stands, if it has any standing left, and I highly doubt that it has."

Tom stood at the front windows of the station, watching as Delaney tucked Regan away in his vehicle and then walked around to slid in himself. Something was niggling at Tom's memory, and that frustrated him that he could not remember. He turned as he heard a voice beside him.

"Abe? When did you get in?"

"Just now. I'm only here to drop this off. Emma insisted it had to be in person. And for the record, I'm glad you're back on their case."

"It just happened. How did you know?"

Abe stared at him. "You didn't know? Your desk officer was very free with that information and he shouldn't have been. He doesn't know me and he shared that with me. He's your leak."

Tom studied the man and then nodded. "I think you're right." He stopped, then grabbed Abe's arm, pulling him outside with him. "Abe, what happened with your investigation of the pharmacist?"

"I gave that information to Angela. Did she not pass it on?"

"No, I didn't see anything there. Tell me."

"You were right. He was running drugs. And he did dispense something different for Regan than what she was told. He's been arrested by another force for fraud and drug dealing. Weren't you told?"

"No, and I don't think any of us knew. This is not good."

Abe nodded and then pointed at his watch. "I have to run. Keep in touch, Tom. If you have any questions or think material is missing, call."

Tom watched as Abe walked away, thoughts racing through his mind before he was running for his vehicle and heading for Delaney and Regan. Something was up there, he knew. She was chased from her house for a reason, and that scared him, tough officer that he was.

Chapter 35

His arm around Regan and feeling Mick shoving against him, Delaney stood, shock on his face, and watched the flames lick at his workshop. He had nothing of real value there anymore, he thought, but he didn't like to see it burn. He felt Regan trembling against him as she watched as well, hands covering her face.

Tom stopped beside them, knowing he didn't need to be there, but had to be. This is what had spurred him to their place.

"What happened, Delaney, other than the obvious?"

Delaney shrugged. "We heard an explosion and when we came out, the workshop was in flames. This should not have happened. I hadn't been working in there. Everything was put away when I was through there this morning."

"Then, someone set it, didn't they? That's why Regan was chased away. They needed to get in and out." He looked around. "The neighbours will be canvased to see if they saw anything, but it's unlikely that they did."

"No, everyone's away at work. The house across the street has a security camera. Talk to them."

Delaney turned Regan finally towards the house, knowing their night was far from over. He could feel the anger beginning to rise in him and then began a fervent prayer for peace and to have the anger released. Regan slumped down into a chair, her hand on Mick, as she watched Delaney move around the kitchen, finally sitting beside her and reaching for her hand.

She opened her mouth and then snapped it closed as she heard him begin to pray, knowing they needed that. She didn't look up as she heard a door open and close and quiet footsteps heading their way. She didn't care anymore. She just wanted to pack up and leave and that wasn't an option.

Delaney finally looked up at his father, who stood in the doorway. "I've had enough, Dad. Regan was threatened all morning and now my shop is gone."

Graeme nodded. "That's why I'm here. Pack some of your things. We're taking you away somewhere. And yes, you can continue to teach. That is a given."

"Who is taking us and what right do you have to make that decision for us?" Regan was on her feet, anger sparking from her as she faced Graeme.

"Tom has asked us to take you somewhere safe. If you don't come with us, he's threatening protective custody until he can find who it is."

Regan stared at him, her mouth open, before she spun to face Delaney, who was watching with interest the battle between the two. She shook her head, a dark look on her face, as she studied him.

"I am not leaving, Delaney. You can go if you want. I have had enough. No more hiding. No more running. They only find us, don't they? So what good is it to be somewhere else?"

Delaney reached for her, wrapping her tight in a hug as he stared at his father before shaking his head.

"She's right, Dad. No more running. As she said, they find us. And I would like to know how?"

"That's what Riordan is working on. He's sending Redmond and Ryanne our way by morning. He said you'd refuse to go. He would do the same."

"They can't come. It's too dangerous." Regan was adamant she didn't want her family around.

"It's past that, Regan. They will be here. That's a given. It's time you accepted their help. You give and give yourself. That's what I've been told. You go beyond what you need to with your family and ask for nothing in return. This time, it's your turn for them to give to you. Rory and Reilly are doing more research. Reilly seemed to think he was on the line of something. And yes, before you ask, he has reached to Emma or it was the other way around, that I'm not sure of."

Regan leaned back against Delaney, feeling safe and cherished in his arms, but knowing they were at a crisis point.

"I don't want to leave my home." Her words were almost whispered, and both men caught the edge of tears in her voice.

Delaney tightened his hold on his wife, knowing that she had been pushed past her limit and needed this to end. His last conversation with Tom echoed in his mind. Tom was there when things happened. He hated to suspect him but somehow someone was finding them, and he wanted that person caught and dealt with.

"I agree with Regan, Dad. I'm not leaving my home. Whoever this is has proven that they can get to us, no matter where we are. Besides, my research is here, what I need for my classes. I don't have everything on line or saved that way. There is a lot of paperwork that I use."

Graeme nodded. "I agree with you. We need to do something though. Your mother has threatened Tom."

Delaney grinned for a moment, seeing in his mind that very conversation. "And Tom promised to solve this yesterday."

Graeme laughed. "That's exactly what he's done. Now, where do we stand? Regan, you've been working hard on this. Let me take a look at what you have. Maybe these old eyes will see something new in that."

She nodded, but didn't move, staring past Graeme, a thought chasing through her mind.

"Graeme. You know Tom well? I think you know him better that Dad does, is that correct?"

"It is, Regan." He waited for her continue, watching her closely. "Why do you ask?"

"I'm curious about his family. He's related to us, but Dad always left us at home when he and Mom headed this way. He refused to say why. Do you know?"

Graeme sighed, knowing it was up to him to tell her, not her father. "I do. Can we head for your office, son? We may need to do some looking up on the internet, as your mother phrases it."

"Sure, Dad. Just let me grab a tray with our coffee and the sandwiches Regan had made earlier." He looked down at her. "I'm sorry, my love. A picnic supper would have suited me." He turned to the door as a tap came and he headed outside to speak with the investigators, knowing they would tell him it had been a deliberate fire in the shop.

Chapter 37

Delaney paused in the doorway to his office an hour later, watching as his father shuffled through the stack of papers that Regan seemed to have accumulated. He hadn't been aware she had found that much. He set down the tray he had been holding, reaching to take the papers from her hands.

Regan looked up in protest, and then sat back, her eyes on Delaney, seeing the devastation he was trying hard to hide. She knew his workshop had been important to him and that he had spent many hours there. She didn't have to be told that it would take time for him to recover from that. Lord, heal his heart from this. We need Your protection right now. We also need You to provide the answers we've been looking for and not finding.

Delaney handed his father a plate and Graeme looked up in surprise, sitting back to assess his son. He shook his head, knowing they would talk later.

Delancy bit into a sandwich, holding it back to look at it, not recognizing the meat. Regan laughed.

"It's a concoction we make at home. Eat it. You'll like it."

"It is good. I'll let you make it again for me." He grinned at her as she shoved at him with her shoulder. "What have you two discovered?"

"For starters, Eric had more family. I'm not sure if Tom is aware of that or not."

"Dad isn't, I know that." Regan waved her phone. "I sent him a text and he was surprised. He said that just added to their work and what were we up to anyway?"

"He said that, did he? And what are we up to?"

Regan shook her head at Delaney, knowing just what he was up to. "This! Your Dad has gone through this all so rapidly. He must speed read."

"He's a physician. They all do. They go through material and can pick out the important stuff quickly. They have to. Sometimes lives depend on that."

"I get that, Delaney. I'm just envious."

Graeme began to laugh. "I'll teach you, Regan, if you want. Then you can do the same." He looked down at his paperwork. "So, we have Eric with a brother and a sister, likely family for them. Where did you put the chart you had been working on?"

"To your right, on the keyboard. I think that's where you left it."

"You're absolutely right." Graeme stood and began to pace. Delaney recognized the deep look on his father's face, and knew he was connecting something.

"Dad? What are you thinking?"

Graeme spun. "I'm thinking that this is almost over. I have a good idea who it is." He spoke a name, stunning the younger couple. "I can see you're surprised. I was too when I started putting names and places and dates."

"But how do we prove it? It will mean putting ourselves out there, won't it?" Regan was almost in tears, fatigue and stress driving her to that point. She rose as she heard the doorbell, muttering that her home had become a bus station, and she had no desire to live in one.

Delaney bit back a laugh, knowing Regan didn't mean her words, but he agreed. The people in and out of their home that night had stressed him out. He glanced down at his feet, spotting Mick on guard, his head up, watching where Regan had gone.

The men looked up in surprise as Regan returned, Redmond and Ryanne behind her.

"You're a day early, you two. You weren't supposed to be here until tomorrow."

"Dad sent us tonight. He seemed to think we were needed." Redmond glanced around the room. "I would say you three have been busy."

"We have been. We have it all figured out. We don't need your help. You're too late." Regan smirked at her siblings, hearing them groan.

"Not so fast. Dad sent more material. Rory and Reilly have been shooting emails at me so fast I can't read one before I have two or three more."

"Tell them to stop. They will. They can combine their findings into fewer emails. That's what I tell them."

"And do they?" Graeme was curious.

"They do. I know their secrets, at least some of them."   Regan's attention was on the stack of material Redmond handed her. "Graeme, this would be a good time for that speed reading lesson."

Graeme laughed. "It would, would it?"

Silence settled down in the room. Delaney finally turned his attention to his class notes for the next day, vaguely hearing the shuffling of papers around him. A crow of triumph had him looking up, watching at Regan and Ryanne hugged.

"This is it, guys. This is it!" Regan was jubilant, almost floating off the couch. "I think we found our culprit. Redmond, you did good. This is your stuff.”

“It is? And what did I find? There was so much stuff I was pulling, I don’t remember what I actually pulled.”

Regan handed him the paper, Delaney rising to stand behind him to read it.

“Her?”

“Her! She’s from here, isn’t she? Lots of money, which is needed to do what she has been. It says here she’s been investigated for drug production but it couldn’t be proven.” Regan sat back, her eyes on the paper. “Ryanne, do you have that report about her family?”

“Here. Why?”

“Because something is odd in it.” She looked up at Graeme. “Graeme, do you know her well?”

He shrugged. “To tell you the truth, none of us do. She’s always been a hidden personality, not sharing with anyone what’s going on. I can see her being the leader, but there has to be someone else. She doesn’t have the knowledge to do something like this.”

Redmond had been listening. “You’re thinking someone in law enforcement or in a legal capacity?”

“Exactly.” Graeme stopped speaking as Delaney made a sound. “Son?”

“And I know who that would be. He’s related to Tom, but not on your side of the family, Regan. He’s very prominent in town, and likes to spread his wealth around, as they say.”

Graeme looked shocked for a moment and then nodded, before he searched through the papers.

"You're right, Delaney. Here is the proof. Regan, you had it all along. We just needed to connect the dots."

"So, where do we go from here? Do we have enough to go to the authorities?"

"Not in proof. We need more."

"Now that we have names, we can look into them closer." Redmond stood, pulling out his phone. "Let me send them on to Rory and Reilly and then Dad."

Chapter 38

Redmond stood and watched, the next morning, as Regan and Ryanne argued back and forth. Regan told him they were not arguing but debating. He had just shrugged and said whatever. He grinned to himself, wondering which one would win the battle this time.

Regan finally jumped to her feet and stalked from the room. Redmond watched, listening for the slamming of the door and not hearing it. He frowned, his eyes going to Ryanne who was still immersed in her papers.

"Ryanne?" When she didn't respond, Redmond walked over, dropping a hand on the papers, causing her to look up. "Ryanne? What was it you two were arguing over anyway?"

Ryanne shrugged. "I have no idea. Regan didn't think we had the right person, even though it seems that way." She leaned back in her chair, a sigh drawn from deep within. "And you know, she is usually right when she gets those feelings."

"This time, I have to agree with her. I don't think we do." Redmond dropped down into a chair, his head turning as he heard footsteps heading his way. "Regan?"

"What?" She snapped at him and then sighed. "I'm sorry. I'm just on edge today and I don't know why. Delaney will be home by one, he says, and I can't wait. I just feel the fury building around us, just like in a hurricane, and that we're soon be swamped."

"I think you're right. I wish I could help you avoid just that, but somehow I know we can't." He looked past her as the doorbell rang. "You did say no one would be around today, didn't you?"

"I did." She spun to stare that way, listening to Mick growling as he paced towards the door. "Redmond! No! Don't! Something's wrong. Mick is alerting and he only does that when there's danger." A scream erupted from her as she faced the door and saw the man standing there. "How did you get in?"

"Easily, my dear. Now, you all will sit. Corral your dog or I'll shoot it."

Regan dropped to the floor, her arms reaching for Mick, holding him despite his attempts to get away from her. She heard Redmond slowing sitting back down.

Ryanne watched, her hand finding her phone, and then sending out a text before she tucked it down under the chair cushion. She just prayed it had gone through. Her eyes stayed on her sister, a slight frown on her face.

Regan watched the man and then the man and woman who walked in behind him, desperation in her eyes. This is it, isn't it, Lord? This is where it ends. Please, comfort my beloved. I know I'm not walking out of here. Protect my siblings. Don't let them die because of me.

Regan sat, trying desperately to come up with a way to get her siblings out of there and not finding a way. Please, Lord, don't let Delaney come into this. I know he would attack them to protect me and that would mean his death. She watched as the men began to pace, the woman finding a seat, her eyes on Regan.

"Who are you?"

The woman gave a jeering laugh. "You'll find out. We have one more person to come and then we'll see how brave you are." She turned her head as she heard the door open and then close and heavy footsteps head their way.

Regan drew in a deep breath. In all her wild dreams, she had not suspected this person. "Wayne Morgan. What a surprise! No wonder you wanted Delaney to teach! That way you could keep track on him. Redmond, Ryanne. Meet the president of the college. And this is his wife, I do believe."

The man smirked at her. "Very good. You finally have made the connection. Unfortunately it will go no further. Once Delaney is here, then we're leaving. Too bad your brother and sister have to suffer because of you."

"That's what I don't get. The why. I didn't meet you until I came here." Her brow wrinkled as she tried to place him from somewhere.

"Oh, but you have. You and your brother." Wayne paced towards her and stopped, looking down at her.

Regan refused to look up. "Which one? I have three."

Redmond grabbed for Mick as he jumped for the man. Regan's hand went to her face, feeling the blood on her fingertip when she touched her mouth. She shook her head, trying to clear it, realizing that baiting the man would only worsen things.

Wayne continued to pace, the words spewing from his mouth, shaking off his wife's hand when she tried to stop him.

Regan listened closely, finally realizing that he was telling them exactly what they needed to know. She looked briefly at Redmond, who gave a brief nod. Good, she thought. He's been able to active his voice recorder. I pray they don't find his phone.

Regan finally stood, shoving Mick towards Ryanne who caught the dog into her arms, struggling to hold onto to him.

"This is enough. Delaney's not coming home. It's past time for that." Regan spun in a circle, moving away from the man and towards the windows. "Here, let me open the window for you. It's getting hot in here."

Picking herself up from the floor, she rubbed at her back, glaring at the man who had tackled her and taken her down.

"That was not necessary. I want the window open. It's too hot in here."

"Not happening. You'd open the window and disappear again." Wayne had by this time pulled out a pistol, aiming it at Ryanne. "Keep it up and your sister will be first of your family to die. Can you live with that, as it will be your fault."

Redmond watched closely, knowing that Regan might just bring herself to be shot. He shook his head as she glanced at him and she frowned, a puzzled look on her face. She had heard soft movements in another room, and prayed that Delaney had not come home. She moved slightly to watch Ryanne, who was staring at the woman, bringing Regan's attention to her.

Regan turned to Victoria Morgan, who she now realized was related to Eric. This was the connection they had missed. Of course, they would know where Delaney was on his digs. He had kept in close contact with the college, taking students on digs for one thing. She sighed. Where will it end, Lord? How m will be involved?

She shuddered at the looks that were being shared between the men. She had no idea who the other man was, but he reminded her of a villain in a movie, a heavy, she thought.

She looked up as Wayne stopped in front of her and drew back, alarmed at the hatred on his face.

"Why, Wayne? What did Delaney do to you?"

He shook with rage before he controlled himself. "This has never been about Delaney. He's just been collateral. This has been about you and your family."

"My family? I have no idea what you mean. I don't think we have ever met. Have we, Redmond?"

"Not us, Regan. Dad."

Wayne spun, his pistol now pointed at Redmond. "Very good, young man. You figured it out. Now, would you like to explain it to your sister?"

"No, because I don't know all the details. I always thought your name sounded familiar. Now I know why. Why don't you tell Regan and Ryanne about your daughter."

Chapter 39

Wayne strode across the room towards Redmond. A blow from the end of the pistol had Redmond on the floor, unconscious, as a scream was torn from Ryanne. Regan stared in shock at her brother before her eyes raised to Wayne.

"Why? What did you do that for? He's no danger to you."

"Oh, you see, my dear young lady. You aren't a danger. This is about payback."

"Payback? I'm sorry. I don't understand."

A hand on her arm dragged her back to a chair and she was shoved roughly down. She could hear the growls from Mick and reached out a hand to touch him, settling him down for the moment.

"Yes, payback." Wayne gave a coarse laugh. "You have no idea that I know your father or why."

"No, we don't. Perhaps you would like to explain so we can understand what's been happening and why."

Ryanne stared at her sister, amazed at her coolness and seeming lack of concern, before her eyes narrowed. She's up to something, Lord. Please, protect my sister.

"I would be glad to." Wayne strutted around the room, his overconfidence apparent. "Yes, I do know your father. It goes back many years, to when you were a child. You see, we had a daughter that was kidnapped and taken to another province. Your father was approached by our lawyer, and he agreed to find her and bring her home." He turned a look of such hate on them that both ladies drew in deep breaths, feeling the very evil coming from him.

"Don't beat around the bush, Wayne. Don't be dramatic. This isn't the time for that." Victoria studied the rings on the hand she held out in front of her, her attention on them, not her husband.

"Just shut up!" Wayne's voice was loud and harsh by now. "I'll tell it the way I want to. It doesn't matter , now does it? I'll have my revenge on Stuart. His daughters will pay the price for his negligence."

"I'm sorry? Dad's negligence? What are you talking about?"

"He's never said anything? Never talked about a raid that went wrong? Never tried to show you he covered up his wrongdoing?"

Regan shared another look with Ryanne before glancing down at Redmond, who laid still.

"No, I can't say that he has. Why don't you tell us?" Her calm manner served to enrage the older man, who pointed the pistol at her, his hand shaking.

"That I will. Our daughter, kidnapped at age 18. Taken west. We tracked her down to a town in a western province. The police wouldn't help. Said she was an adult and unless we could prove she had been kidnapped, they could not intervene. That's when we went to your father. Or rather our lawyer did. Your father agreed to bring her home." He raised the pistol once more, pointing it at Regan's head. "He failed. He didn't bring her home. He said she refused to come. There is no way she would have refused to return home."

"I'm sure Dad did his best. If he said she refused, then she refused. It can happen. She was adult. She could make her own decisions. Just how sure were you that she was kidnapped in the first place?"

Enraged, Wayne dragged Regan to her feet, the pistol pointed directly at her temple. He pulled her through the house, despite Ryanne's protests that died away as the other man pointed his own weapon at her.

Shoving Regan out of the door, Wayne shook her, her hair flying loose from the clip she had used. His words were undecipherable due to his rage.

A sudden shout had him spinning around before he caught Regan in a tight grip, the pistol aimed at her heart this time.

Police officers in full riot gear surrounded him. Despite their shouts for him to release Regan, he refused, as he tried to find a way around them, but was unsuccessful. Regan tried to control her whimpers of fear but they escaped her as she frantically tried to think of a way to escape. She suddenly dropped her body, throwing Wayne off balance. As she did, she heard a thud above her and then she was on the ground, Wayne's body trapping her. Hands reached to move him, to pull her to her feet and then rush her away from the area, to the front of the house and to the care of paramedics. She shook, the adrenalin rush fading.

She shook off the hands that were trying to help her, rushing back towards the house before an arm around her stopped. She struggled, crying that her brother and sister were in there. She sobbed that they would be killed. She needed to get to them.

Tom finally just picked her up and carried her away to the ambulance sitting down the street from the house, setting her down on the stretcher and standing in her way, not letting her past.

She glared at him, anger in her manner, before she shook her head.

"Get them out safely, Tom. That's all I ask. Redmond was knocked out. Wayne did that. Please, Lord, let them be okay. Get them out, please Dear Lord." She looked past Tom and then was out and into Delaney's arms, sobs shaking her body as he moved her way and towards where both their parents stood. Riordan reached to hug her before Naomi had her in her arms. Morag's arm was around Delaney as she watched the house.

A sudden shout broke out from the house, sending fear through them all. Finally, Tom walked towards them, his arm around Ryanne.

"Tom? Redmond?" Riordan's worried voice carried through the darkening night.

"He's on his feet. A paramedic is heading out with him and taking him to the hospital. Just as a precaution. Here, Ryanne. Your parents are here."

Riordan walked off with Tom, Graeme with them, as the family members watched. Was it over, they wondered? And just what had happened?

Regan clung to Delaney, shudders still running through her. His arms tight around her, he watched, knowing they would hear soon what had happened. He watched too as Victoria Morgan and their henchman were brought out and shoved roughly into vehicles before they were taken away.

Chapter 40

Accepting a plate of food with thanks, Tom turned to face the living room at Delaney's, seeing all of Riordan's family there as well as Graeme's. He sighed. He wished this had never happened, that Delaney and Regan had not had to go through what they did. He looked up briefly, asking for help from above to finally explain what remained. He didn't like what he had learned. He could only imaging how Riordan was feeling, knowing that this went back all those years. Riordan had confided in him that Regan had been four when this happened. To think that Wayne had plotted this all those years. Riordan had shaken his head and walked away, his shoulders stooped, sorrow in his heart.

"Tom?" He heard Regan speaking from beside him and turned to look down at her, seeing compassion on her face. "It's not your fault. You wouldn't, couldn't have known. No one did. He hid it well. Did you know about his daughter?"

He shook his head. "No. They kept it quiet that she had left, only saying she had decided to move away and take work somewhere else." He looked up at Delaney. "I'm sorry, Delaney. If I had known, I would have taken steps."

Delaney shrugged. "No one I've had come up to me and say anything had any inkling of what he was really like. I mean, he wasn't all that well liked. The rumour is that he bought his way into the college and to the presidency of it."

"Those rumours would be correct. He hid so much." Tom sank into a chair, fatigue from the last week of long hours weighing him down. He looked down at his plate, knowing he needed to eat, but knowing they needed to hear what he had to say. He looked up again as he felt a presence beside him.

Riordan sat beside his cousin, knowing how they were both feeling. "Eat, Tom. You need it. Then, we spend time in prayer. We need that. We need to find the presence of God and find His comfort and peace. That's what will help us get through the next bit." He nodded at Delaney and Regan. "Those two have found peace and comfort both in God and in each other." He watches his daughter as she laughed at her husband's comments to Reilly, content and safe in the circle of his arm. "They have been through a lot. Regan said she felt the fury of the storm and that it almost overwhelmed her, but she remembered that she was His who calmed the storm and that calmed her."

Tom chewed slowly as he thought about her words before he swallowed. "She's right, you know. Three of yours have been through storms we wouldn't have wished on them, but they came through stronger and all found the life mates God meant for them."

He finally set his plate aside, watching as Graeme stood and began to pray, then leaving it open for whoever wanted to pray. A sense of God's presence almost overwhelmed Regan and she shivered at the wonder of it, Delaney's arms tightening around her.

Tom finally stood, his eyes searching each one before he began to speak. Most of what he had to say, they already knew.

"Regan, I'm sorry I didn't know before and prevented this. It was when he saw you with Delaney on that dig that he decided he needed to exact revenge on your Dad. He was the one who had that photo taken, the one who set up the bomb scare, the one who had you kidnapped both times and the two of you that once. He destroyed your workshop, Delaney, as a threat towards you, to send you into the open more so he could get to Regan through you. That didn't work.

"The drug you were taking, Regan? It was a synthetic drug, new to the street, but he had it changed in formula enough that it affected you the way it did. He's been the one behind the drugs in this town. He hid that well. We would catch dealers but they never told on him. He had dealers killed as a warning to others.

"The pharmacist? He was being blackmailed. That is a confidential matter right now as to why, but it will come out in court at some point.

"Riordan, he had it in for you. He did blame you that his daughter refused to come home, unable to accept the fact that she felt she had escaped for a horrendous situation and refused to have anything to do with her parents at any time.

"Victoria was involved all the way. Hers is the voice you heard, Regan. The man you heard in the hospital, that was their bodyguard. Somehow he was able to get in to your room, likely when you were taken out for an imaging study. Security found a microphone that was used by him. So you really did hear someone. His voice sounded close to your surgeon, which is why you were confused as to who it was.

"Delaney, your position at the college? Wayne arranged for that, to keep an eye on you. We have no idea why other than he was jealous of your success. We found documentation that he planned to accuse you of fraud on the last dig. Somehow he connected you and Regan."

Delaney nodded. "That woman you couldn't find a proper name for? She became his assistant. So now you can speak with her. She's in there with them in their criminal activity." He turned to look at Riordan and Naomi. "I understand now why you refused to bring your family here. You stopped doing that about the time he accused you of not finding his daughter. Is that correct?"

Riordan nodded. "That's right, Delaney. We never felt safe bringing the family here after that, not even when they were adults. I never said, but every couple of years, I would receive a letter from him, filled with accusations. Tom, I'll turn them over to you. There was nothing in them that I could use to file charges."

"Thank you, Riordan. That will help explain things. He made his choice at the end, Regan. You could not talk him out of what he did. I know you tried, that's your character. He has gone on to face a higher judge. I am just so thankful that you are both okay."

"He's the one, isn't he? The one who called in the bomb threat? I don't understand why."

"Victoria couldn't wait to blame him. Apparently he had this idea that if he called in a bomb threat he could get to Delaney and through him to you. He got you instead. She said he left you alone at times and played the voices and music to try and drive you to instability. That didn't work. He did have you drugged at those times as well with a mild sedative. His revenge has steeped over the years in his mind. What he would have done, we have no idea. Victoria is not saying, if she knows."

Tom looked around the room once more, thankful that everyone was safe. He watched as Delaney and Regan shared a look and then conversed with their families. He slipped away, knowing he had paperwork waiting, but for once, he needed to be counselled himself. His minister was waiting for him to come and talk it through.

Epilogue

A month later, Delaney searched the house for Regan, not finding her. He headed for the outside, not seeing Mick either. He began to search harder before he heard the singing coming from the area of his new workshop. She had insisted he needed to rebuild it, that he would need it for future artifacts from future digs. The building was enclosed but still needed the windows and doors.

He paused in the doorway, leaning against the opening, his eyes on her as she paced the room. He knew what she was up to. She was organizing him. She had laughingly told him that was her task now.

Mick gave a low woof and moved towards him, his tail wagging. Delaney bent to greet him and then stood upright again, finding Regan standing in the middle of the room, her eyes on him, a smile on her face.

He moved towards her as she moved towards him, wrapping her into a tight hug before he kissed her thoroughly. She laid her head against his chest, listening to his heart beat, knowing that her world was sane and just right once more.

"Mrs. Callahan, may I interest you in a picnic supper and then a walk along the lake shore? And yes, Mick can come."

"I like that idea. We never did get that picnic supper we planned all those weeks ago."

"I know." He reached for her head, heading for his car, opening the door to let her in and watching as Mick jumped in as well and then over her to the back seat where he spun, to stand with his chin on her shoulder. "I still think I've lost my dog."

“No, he shares us.”

He laughed as he started the car and pulled away from their home. “He shares you more than he does me. But that’s okay.”

Dusk had dropped by the time they were standing near the lake, having walked the shoreline and back, arms around each other.

“I was so scared that day, my love. I thought I had lost you. I didn’t think you would survive.” Delaney’s arm tightened around her.

“I know. I thought the same. I was so afraid that he had killed Redmond. And when he pulled me from the room, I didn’t know if Ryanne would live. God has been good. He kept His promises to keep us safe.”

“That He did. We will have an adventure to thrill our children and grandchildren someday.”

“That we will. On another note, Delaney, I think I know what I want to do. I want to set up some kind of network or charity for girls at risk. I think that is where God is leading. I haven’t worked it all out yet.”

“We’ll pray it out, my love. We will do that. I think it’s a wonderful plan. You have experience that you can share.” He looked down at her. “Have I told you today how much I love you?”

“You have, but I can always hear it again. And I love you too. I think that was the hardest part of this, knowing how much we loved each other but being afraid to speak of it. We were so worried that what we were going through would tear us apart.”

“And it could so easily have done that. God allowed this to happen. He was leading us, although sometimes it was too dark to see where we were headed. You told your Dad, I believe, that you felt you had experienced the fury of a storm. That is a good way to describe it. We went through a storm, knowing who calms them, and He did just that.”

Her head against his chest, his heart beating strong and steady in her ear, she agreed.

Dear Readers:

Thank you for choosing to read Through The Fury of The Storm. Once more, the characters drove the storyline. I had no idea where they were heading or who would be involved or why. All I knew what that they were going through a storm and only the One who calms the storms could save them. They had to rely on His protection as they faced their foes.

We all face storms of some kind or other. Some are more furious than others. We are never in them alone. God is there in the midst of them. He brings in friends and even strangers that help us face them.

A picture I always have of a storm is seeing a ship beaten by the waves, but still rising and falling with them, staying upright. We may be battered and bruised by life, but we have the confidence that God loves us and protects us.

God bless.

Ronna